Garrett could almost feel his daughter's arms wrapped around his own neck.

He watched as Annie put her down. The image of his little girl waving goodbye as the door closed burned itself into his head.

When he met Annie back at her house, the first thing out of her mouth was, "Your Megan is absolutely adorable. She's just wonderful."

"How was she?" he asked. "I mean, did she seem…happy?"

"She seemed good, Garrett. Happy, affectionate."

He nodded, looking over her shoulder, swallowing the sudden lump in his throat. Annie touched his chin and he met her gaze. "She squealed and hugged herself when she thought of you," she added.

He smiled slowly, a bittersweet, tear-at-the-heart kind of smile. He had a lot to make up to his little girl. How had every good intention he had turned out to be wrong?

He had to get Megan back. There was absolutely no other option.

ALICE SHARPE
BODYGUARD FATHER

HARLEQUIN®

TORONTO • NEW YORK • LONDON
AMSTERDAM • PARIS • SYDNEY • HAMBURG
STOCKHOLM • ATHENS • TOKYO • MILAN • MADRID
PRAGUE • WARSAW • BUDAPEST • AUCKLAND

This book is dedicated to Elisabeth Naughton and
Lisa Pulliman, roommates extraordinaire

ISBN-13: 978-0-373-88856-6
ISBN-10:   0-373-88856-2

BODYGUARD FATHER

www.eHarlequin.com

Printed in U.S.A.

ABOUT THE AUTHOR

Alice Sharpe met her husband-to-be on a cold, foggy beach in Northern California. One year later they were married. Their union has survived the rearing of two children, a handful of earthquakes registering over 6.5, numerous cats and a few special dogs, the latest of which is a yellow Lab named Annie Rose. Alice and her husband now live in a small rural town in Oregon, where she devotes the majority of her time to pursuing her second love, writing.

Alice loves to hear from readers. You can write her at P.O. Box 755, Brownsville, OR 97327. SASE for reply is appreciated.

Books by Alice Sharpe

HARLEQUIN INTRIGUE
746—FOR THE SAKE OF THEIR BABY
823—UNDERCOVER BABIES
923—MY SISTER, MYSELF*
929—DUPLICATE DAUGHTER*
1022—ROYAL HEIR
1051—AVENGING ANGEL
1076—THE LAWMAN'S SECRET SON**
1082—BODYGUARD FATHER**

*Dead Ringer
**Skye Brother Babies

CAST OF CHARACTERS

Garrett Skye—Accused of killing the woman he was paid to protect, he's on the run. His goals: recover from the wound sustained in his escape, regain custody of his three-year-old daughter and disappear forever.

Anastasia (Annie) Ryder—This cookie-baking preschool teacher turns down her private detective father's last attempt at reconciliation. Can she atone for her behavior by completing his last case: finding Garrett Skye?

Megan Skye—This three-year-old charmer is the center of Garrett's heart. He'll do anything to protect her....

Shelby Greason—She hired Annie's father to bring her mother's killer to justice.

Robert Greason—Still grief stricken by his wife's death, he's now receiving death threats of his own.

"Curly" and "Moe"—Two thugs with deadly intent.

Rocko Klugg—Awaiting a new trial, everyone knows he's a murderer and that he wanted Elaine Greason dead. But what is he looking for now and how far will he go to get it?

Jasmine Carrabas—Klugg's girlfriend. This slick beauty has a scary mean streak.

Randy Larson (Red Thunder)—Have his dreams corrupted him?

Tiffany Boothe Skye—Garrett's ex. Her interest in being a mother is less than her interest in a new man. How far will she go to destroy Garrett's credibility?

Ellen Boothe—Tiffany's mother, Megan's reluctant babysitter.

Brady Skye—Garrett's older brother is a lawman in Oregon. Will he help or hinder his brother's efforts to clear his name?

Lara Skye—Brady's beloved wife, the sister Annie never had.

Chapter One

Annie Ryder was ready to call it quits. Two days of lurking around in the cold, snapping pictures of old buildings, old streets and old ranchers had left her stiff and grumpy. Plus, the unfamiliar black-framed glasses rested heavy on the bridge of her nose while the thick brown wig atop her head itched to the point of distraction.

Oh, who was she trying to fool? Or, worse, impress? "You can't impress a dead man," she mumbled to herself.

A badly tuned engine jerked her from her thoughts. She peered down the street in time to spot a beat-up blue truck approaching. She didn't need to consult the photograph in her pocket to know at long last this was *the* truck—and hopefully the driver—she'd been waiting for. Round bumpers, dented hood, broken antenna, a faded Forty-Niners bumper sticker, California plates. This was it.

Hallelujah…

Lifting the camera, she flexed numb fingers. "Stop at the grocery store," she whispered as she watched the truck ramble down the road.

For a second, she thought it would pass by and her stomach twisted into a knot that just as quickly unraveled as the truck pulled to the curb no more than ten feet from where she stood concealed in an alley. The driver got out of the truck and without locking his door or glancing back at Annie's location, limped across the road toward the grocery store on the corner. He wore faded blue jeans and a black jacket. Worn leather cowboy boots looked like the real deal.

He reached into his left pocket, emerged with an old fashioned gold watch that he snapped open, glanced at and snapped shut. He dug a few coins from his other pocket.

Annie raised the camera and peered through the lens, zooming in on his face. She found the chiseled features she'd appreciated in his photo, more obvious now that he'd shaved off the mustache he'd worn before. His hair was darker and scruffier though without the facial hair; he looked younger than his thirty-three years.

Garrett Skye, at last.

She zeroed in on his eyes and for a second, he seemed to look right at her. Her breath caught in alarm, but that quickly evaporated. He had amazing deep-brown eyes, warm and sensual, even when viewed through a lens. Eyes that reminded her of the old "windows of the soul" malarkey, eyes that brimmed with self-awareness, eyes that skated on the razor-thin edge of magic.

She lowered the camera a fraction of an inch and stared back at him, unable to move. His gaze should strike fear in the bottom of her heart. It didn't.

This was nuts. Those beautiful eyes belonged to a man who killed without remorse. No doubt his last victim had thought she saw humanity in those deep, dark irises, too. Well, that woman was dead now, thanks to him, so get a grip!

His gaze shifted. Obviously, he was just looking around, being cautious. He slid a few coins into the paper machine and snagged a copy. Annie quickly snapped the first of a dozen photos before he disappeared into the store.

She hurriedly reinvented what she'd seen through the camera lens. Not warmth, not beauty. Cockiness, smugness, vanity, that's what she'd seen. He thought he was safe. He hadn't counted on the dead woman's grown daughter having deep pockets and a vengeful nature. He hadn't counted on Annie's late father's detective skills.

And he hadn't counted on her, Annie Ryder, intrepid preschool teacher/unofficial private eye.

Her job was simple: verify Garrett Skye's presence, learn what name he was using, get an address in Poplar Gulch, tell the client.

She drew only a cursory glance from two women as she stepped out of the alley and snapped a few random pictures of the hay bales in the back of Skye's truck to reinforce her cover story as an out-of-town photographer writing a book on forgotten ranching towns. She paused. Dare she risk frisking the glove box?

A brisk "Good morning" from a passing pedestrian sent Annie's heart leaping into her throat. She settled on taking a few photos of the mail scattered on the front seat while moving past the truck.

She continued walking to the next block where she'd parked her father's white sedan. The weatherman had predicted snow. Annie wanted to be out of Poplar Gulch and headed home to Reno by the time it fell. All she needed now was a physical address for Skye.

She'd just set the camera on the seat beside her when movement in the side mirror drew her attention. Skye limped back across the street, the newspaper tucked beneath his arm, a small plastic grocery bag swinging from the fingers of his left hand. He opened the driver's door, tossed in his purchases and climbed in after them.

She started her own engine, a blast of cold air

coming from the heater vent making her shiver. Skye made a U-turn and headed east. Annie waited a few moments before making the same turn and following at a distance. Golden strands of hay floated out of the back of the truck.

Within minutes, it had started to rain, drops icy enough to make patterns on her windshield. With no vehicle between her and the truck, Annie lowered her visor and stayed as far back as possible. Skye had been on the run for almost four months, surely he'd be feeling pretty comfortable by now. On the other hand, the man was former military, former bodyguard and a wanted killer. Plus, he apparently knew a thing or two about explosives.

He drove for a couple of miles before taking a sharp left onto a dirt road that appeared to lead up a heavily forested hillside. Annie drove past the road, making note of the mailbox on which the name *B. Miller* was printed, pulling off a quarter mile farther along, parking well off the shoulder. Miller. She recognized the name from her father's files. He was connected to Skye in some way. An old army buddy, that was it.

Another tidbit of information floated into her mind. Miller was a professor at Davis University, currently out of the country on a sabbatical. She'd bet big money Garrett Skye was using his old buddy's mountain retreat as a hideout!

Excited, she clicked on her cell phone, relieved when it picked up a signal, disappointed when the client didn't answer. She waited through Shelby Parker's recorded message and left one of her own, embellishing it a little here and there to make it sound better, making sure Parker understood Annie was working with her father. No reason to mention the fact he had died before he could complete this job. No point in admitting she was his proxy.

As she clicked off the phone it dawned on her she should have made sure Skye was living here before alerting the client. She turned off the cell phone and tucked it and her father's nasty-looking black gun in her pockets. She looped the camera strap around her neck. She stuck her purse under the seat and got out of the car, locking it behind her.

The walk in, which she had assumed would be relatively short, turned out to be more than a mile straight up. It seemed to grow colder with each foot she climbed. The rain was still halfhearted, but it had the icy punch of coming trouble.

The road ended so abruptly she stumbled into the open. Quickly dodging behind a gaggle of leafless, wispy trees, she took in the old house across from what appeared to be an even older barn. Tucked between them sat the rusty blue truck, its bed now empty.

Annie took the camera from around her neck. Snapping pictures of anything that didn't move, her bare fingers growing increasingly numb as the temperature continued to plummet, she made her way to the back of the barn where she discovered a two-tiered door, the top of which was open.

She knelt with her head below the door opening, catching her breath, nerves firing up and down her spine. A moment later, a blast of hot air came from above. Annie jumped an inch off the ground, grabbing her wig with one hand while fumbling for the gun with the other. The camera tumbled to the ground in the process. Before she could extract the gun from her pocket, she looked up and came eyeball to muzzle with a big brown horse.

She swallowed what felt like her heart. "Easy does it," she whispered, fear draining out of her as she reached up to shoo away the warm nose nibbling at her wig. The horse tossed its head and whinnied.

"Shh," she said, turning to peer around the side of the barn.

She found two worn leather boots she immediately recognized. The rifle, however, was new.

"Get up nice and easy," Garrett Skye said, his voice as cold as the steel barrel nine inches from her nose.

As distasteful as Annie found carrying a gun, looking up the barrel of one was worse. Way worse.

Scooping the camera from the icy mud, she gained her feet. Up close and without the distancing lens of the camera, the man was big, muscular, powerful and scary. His chiseled good looks were a mere distraction compared to the focused intent in his eyes. There was no appealing warmth or humor in those irises now. There probably never had been.

"Who are you?" he said, his voice deep, softer than she'd expected, and scary. Everything about him was scary. Rip up his clothes a little, tie a bandana around his head and a knife between his teeth and, presto, Rambo in the flesh.

Annie thought frantically. She hadn't had a chance to pull out her dad's gun. Perhaps Skye would overlook it. She babbled, "Is this your place? I'm so sorry to be intrusive, my car broke down on the main road and yours was the nearest driveway. I'm in Poplar Gulch taking pictures of forgotten ranch towns. This place is perfect. Uh, I love your horse. What's its name?"

"Your car broke down?" he said, narrowing his eyes.

"Yes. It's old and—"

"So you didn't follow me out here?"

"Follow you? No. Of course not."

He stared at her for another second or two and then shook his head. "Sorry, not buying it. I'll take your gun."

"I don't have a gun, Mr. Miller, isn't it?"

"You know damn good and well my name isn't Miller and of course you have a gun. Get your hands up. Who sent you here? Klugg?"

"Klugg who?" she muttered.

"I said, get your hands up."

She put her hands up in the air, the camera clenched tight in her right fist, the strap dangling down her arm. With a few swift impersonal strokes he frisked her with his free hand, finding the gun and her cell phone with no trouble. The picture of his truck taken a week or so before rolled out with them.

Even if she could think of a way to explain carrying a gun, there was no way to make this look like an accident now, not with that picture waiting to be unfolded. Icy calm spread through her fear-soaked body. She grew quiet, watchful, waiting…

Flipping the gun open, he spun the chamber and a couple of bullets popped out. "No gun, huh?" he quipped, sparing her an uneasy glance. He closed the chamber with his thumb and stuck the gun in his pocket before unfolding the photograph.

In the moment it took him to do this, he was marginally distracted. Annie threw the camera at his face and without waiting for his reaction, took off around the far side of the barn, expecting to hear the sharp retort of his rifle….

But it was his voice that followed her. Loud, angry, ordering her to stop. *Sure.* The horse whinnied his opinion of the mayhem.

Annie veered toward the truck, hoping Skye was in the habit of leaving his keys in the ignition. He wasn't. Leaping the two feet onto the broad front porch of his house, she tore open the front door and locked it behind her. The small kitchen hosted a back door. As she touched the knob, she heard the tinkle of broken glass coming from the front. Skye would be inside within seconds. She ran outside, circling by the barn again. He'd see her if she took off down the road and there wasn't a doubt in her mind that he could run faster, even with a limp, than she could.

And bullets ran faster than either of them.

That left the horse. She ducked into the barn, faltering for a second as her eyes fought to adjust to the shadows, almost tripping over the bales of hay Skye had apparently unloaded just inside the door. She ran toward the only light, the open half door through which the horse had spotted her. There was no purpose hiding in a dark corner—he'd find her. She could see no handy weapon and doubted she'd be able to throw a pitchfork hard enough to stop him anyway.

She'd take the horse and ride it down the

mountain and escape that way. Good Lord, what was she thinking?

She was thinking she didn't want to die.

She approached the animal as slowly as her panic and pounding heart allowed. The big brown horse eyed her suspiciously as she opened his stall door. He was a lot bigger than he'd looked from the outside when the business half of him had been obscured by the lower half of the door. She didn't have time to get to know him or even saddle him. Any minute now, Garrett Skye would erupt through that door wielding his rifle—

She stretched out a hand to touch the horse's glistening neck, surprised at his warmth. He was wearing a halter but his head was a long way from his back even when he twisted around and looked her eyeball to eyeball. She half expected him to ask her what the hell she thought she was doing. She grabbed a handful of fetlock and bounced on her feet to build the momentum to swing herself atop.

As she launched herself upward, Skye limped his way through the barn door, his rifle held at his side. For a second, Annie imagined Skye's shocked expression when she proceeded to gallop the brown horse right over the top of him.

The horse rose up partly on his hind legs, twisted around and thudded back to the earth. Annie went flying as her tenuous grip failed.

Her last conscious thought was irritation with herself, not the horse. Then she hit the wall and slid to the floor, the world eclipsed to a single black dot and then to nothing....

Chapter Two

Setting the rifle aside, Garrett put a steady hand on Scio's nose. "It's okay, fella," he whispered as he ran a hand along the horse's quivering flesh. He carefully led the nervous animal out of the stall so he wouldn't trample their intruder. He put him in an adjoining stall and closed the gate.

His mind moved faster than his body as he returned to the woman. He had to assume she had called in Klugg's men or the police, depending on which side of the law she worked. If it was the police they'd already be here. That left Klugg and that meant he had three or four hours to get as far away from here as possible. Besides the horse, everything of any importance was already packed in a duffel bag and stowed behind the bench seat in Ben's truck. If there was one thing Garrett knew how to do it was cut his losses and move on. He'd drive to the nearest big city and abandon the truck there, as per his long planned escape route.

First things first. What in the world did he do with the woman in Scio's stall?

She wasn't very big and she wasn't very old, maybe mid-twenties. Her black glasses had come loose and he plucked them from the stable floor. He peered through the lenses—no correction— and tossed them aside.

Balancing on the balls of his feet, he squatted beside her, his right leg aching with the movement. He was reassured to find a pulse fluttering in her throat. All he needed was another dead woman on his hands.

The thick brown hair sat kind of lopsided on her head. As he watched, it slid to the ground and lay there like a dead squirrel, revealing finely textured lustrous auburn hair pinned atop her head, held with a bunch of little pink-and-yellow butterfly clips. The kind his kid wore. They looked sweet on Megan. On a grown woman they made a disconcerting statement he wouldn't even try to figure out.

What in the world should he do with her? Man, he should have shot her when she threw the damn camera at him, but he didn't shoot unarmed people in the back.

Not even hired hit men.

Is that what she was? She hadn't had her gun ready, she hadn't planned an escape and she was wearing little butterflies in her hair. He patted her down, ignoring the tantalizing bumps and curves under her clothing, and came away empty-handed. But he was also pretty sure nothing was broken or bleeding and that was a relief.

Also, no identification, just one car key dangling on a ring. As far as he was concerned, that fit the profile of a pro, and a hardened one at that. Of course there was her phone to take a look at, but first he needed to figure out what to do with her.

He lifted one of her eyelids with his thumb and she groaned. He fetched a coil of rope from a hook on the wall and, using his pocketknife, sliced it into lengths. He tied her hands together in front of her, then her ankles. No need for a gag; there was no one on this hill to hear her except Scio and himself. With a sigh, he unceremoniously flopped her over his shoulder and carried her back into the cabin. He dumped her in a big chair by the fire before stoking the dying embers and tossing on another log. Standing with his back to the comforting warmth, he ignored the pain in his leg and stared at her.

In the quick trip between the barn and the house, she'd collected a few of the predicted snowflakes on her silky hair. They melted as he watched. It had been a long time since he'd been close to a woman. A long time. He'd almost forgotten the yielding softness of a female body, the fragrance of perfumed hair. This woman looked deceptively sweet and innocent. Dark lashes against pale cheeks, lips slightly parted and faintly peach-colored. In another time and place, he would have enjoyed just looking at her.

He turned away abruptly and left the cabin, closing the door behind him. He'd broken a pane of glass in the top of the door to get inside when he chased her. He'd have to repair that before he left Ben's cabin.

First he veered toward the barn, where he retrieved the camera she'd thrown at him. Then he went into the barn to reassure the horse and reclaim his rifle. As he made his way down the hill, snowflakes gathering on his bare head and shoulders, he reviewed the last several pictures she'd taken—the driveway, the barn and house, Ben's junk mail, several of him in front of Naughton's Stop and Shop.

She was after him, all right.

When he dug for the car key he'd confiscated, he came across the photo of his truck, the one he'd found in her pocket when he searched for her gun. It took him a moment to figure out where the picture had been taken. The broken antenna placed it within the last month. He was sitting alone in the cab, staring out the driver's-side window. He wore an old green hat he'd found in the barn.

He'd worn that hat only once and that had been during a quick trip to Reno to catch a glimpse of Megan. Back around her birthday in early December. His daughter's smile had warmed his heart for the past several days, but if it meant he'd put her in danger, the cost had been too high and he swore at himself.

He knew why his intruder hadn't trailed him back from Reno that day. There'd been a terrible road accident right behind him, one involving a semi and two cars. Though he'd sailed away from it, the traffic behind had come to a dead halt.

He wadded up the picture and stuffed it back in his pocket. Life had gotten so damn complicated. In the past, he would have kept running right out of the country if need be. The problem would have gone away because he would have reinvented himself somewhere else. No ties meant mobility.

But now there was Megan to consider.

He finally reached the road. No sign of the car. She must have driven past and parked it up around the bend. His leg was killing him and he swore softly. Why hadn't she just driven up the damn hill?

A quarter of a mile later, he rounded a turn to find an older white sedan with Nevada license plates. Using her keys, he unlocked the car and slid behind the wheel. The car was registered to someone named Jack Ryder. A hasty search of the glove box revealed a few folded maps. He felt under the seat and came out with a woman's woven handbag. It held little more than a small zipped wallet. The driver's license showed his visitor's face. Her name was Anastasia Ryder. So, was she Jack Ryder's wife? She had a credit card, a library card and grocery store discount card. No private-eye license. A few receipts fell out of a side pocket. She had purchased new shoes and two different wigs three days before in Reno.

He also found a plastic bag half full of what looked like homemade oatmeal cookies and a key attached to a green oval labeled *Shut Eye Inn, rm. 7,* the sole motel in town.

Remembering the cell phone he confiscated, he dug it from a pocket, turned it on and scrolled through the outgoing calls. None to a local number. The last one she made was to an area code he didn't recognize, but that wasn't surprising. There were hundreds of new area codes now thanks to the proliferation of cell phones. The call had been made an hour before he caught Anastasia Ryder behind Scio's barn. He pushed the call button. The phone was answered by a recording.

A woman's voice. Name of Shelby Parker. He didn't recognize her voice but her name rang a distant bell. No, he couldn't remember where he'd heard it before. Was she connected to Rocko Klugg?

He flipped the phone closed and rubbed his jaw with cold fingers, trying to figure things out. At least Anastasia hadn't called the police. And if her appearance was connected to Klugg, it would take hours for his henchmen to get here.

In the end, did it matter who Anastasia Ryder worked for? She carried a gun and a picture of him taken outside his ex-wife's house. She'd taken photos of everything connected to him. Obviously, someone had employed Ms. Ryder to track him down and she had.

Driving her car, he made a U-turn on the empty road and drove back up his driveway, his leg screaming in protest as he hit every rut in the dirt road. The weather had grown even colder, the road icier. As he neared the top, his tires fell into well-worn grooves. If not for them, he'd skid all over the place. He flipped on the windshield wipers as snow started to fly.

And then he saw it. His truck, aimed right at him, barreling down the hillside, his prisoner at the wheel. He'd left the damn keys on a hook by the door!

For an instant, he met Anastasia Ryder's green-eyed gaze as he slammed on the brakes, sending pain shooting up his right leg. He yanked the wheel to the left but she kept coming, the truck's momentum overriding its aging brakes, sending it into a death skid aimed right at him.

The truck hit the car starting at the front right fender and grinding its way down the body, crushing the doors with a horrible metal on metal sound until it imbedded itself into what had once been the trunk. The car stopped abruptly thanks to a tree and that jarring conclusion saved him an uncomfortable trip down the hillside. It also released the air bag and he sank into it instead of slamming against the steering wheel.

Shaking inside, Garrett took inventory. Besides his leg, remarkably, everything else seemed to be in working order. He fought off the air bag, took the keys from the ignition and dumped them in Annie's purse. After wrenching open his door, he slipped and slid his way around the car.

Ben's truck was history. Radiator pushed inward, hood buckled, steam hissing, windshield shattered…it wasn't going anywhere again. Damn, neither was the car. The two locked vehicles made a dandy roadblock.

How did Anastasia Ryder get untied? Stupid question, he knew how. He hadn't tied her tight enough, he hadn't wanted to break her soft skin. He hadn't wanted to yank her arms behind her, he hadn't wanted to hurt her.

And in payment of this gentle treatment, she crashed his getaway truck.

He pulled open the truck door, dreading what

he would find. Anastasia had been thrown or had thrown herself flat onto the bench seat and she sat up slowly, her lovely face splattered with her own blood, hair tumbling across her forehead and down her shoulders. Tiny cubes of safety glass sparkled in her hair like ice crystals.

Her hands were still tied together, a cut rope dangled from the knot around one ankle. She'd apparently used his biggest kitchen knife to cut her feet free and brought it along as a possible weapon. It now stuck straight out from the dashboard, the tip imbedded in vinyl, the plastic handle still vibrating from the impact.

She bit her lip when her gaze followed his and she saw the knife.

"You're lucky it didn't imbed itself in something softer. Like your throat," he said.

She nodded in a dazed kind of fashion.

"Can you move?"

She nodded again and sat perfectly still, blinking.

"I'll help you," he said.

More nodding. He brushed some of the glass away then reached inside and pulled on her jacket sleeve and her jeans. She slid closer to the edge of the seat until she slipped into his arms as though she belonged there. She looped her arms over his head and around his neck and for a second, he wondered if she knew how to choke a man with a rope. But instead of trying to strangle him, she looked into his eyes. The cold, miserable day receded, the pain ebbed, the clock stopped ticking.

"Thanks," she said, lowering her gaze.

"If you'd stayed tied up this wouldn't have happened," he grumbled as he carried her away from the hissing, steaming mass of mangled metal. He set her on her feet, anxious to see just how injured she was. She swayed a little but caught herself.

"Can you walk?" he barked.

"Of course," she said, shaking glass off her clothes, out of her hair. "I'm just a little…rattled," she added, and proved it by trembling from the feet up.

"Stand here for a second," he said as he handed her her handbag. "Don't run away."

He limped back to the truck and grabbed the rifle before pulling his duffel bag from behind the seat. He didn't know how he was going to get out of here now that both vehicles were wrecked, but he knew he had to. Soon.

She still stood where he'd left her. What was he going to do with her? He couldn't leave her here alone, could he? He pulled out his pocket watch and checked the time. The minutes kept ticking by.

As he approached, he saw the return of fear in her eyes. Why she should be afraid of him when it was she who had started this mess?

She believes you blew up Elaine Greason.

He moved a few steps toward the house and looked back at her. "Let's go inside while I come up with plan B."

She looked anxiously over his shoulder toward the cabin and back again, her gaze straying past the wreck. It appeared she longed to run down the hill screaming at the top of her lungs.

"The snow is beginning to stick," he said.

"But—"

"Listen. I know you're Anastasia Ryder, I know you have a husband named Jack, I know you came to find me and that you called someone named Shelby Parker once you followed me back to Ben's place. I know all this. I know you've been stalking me and I know why. So let's can the scared female act. Thanks to your little escape attempt, I have to figure out how I'm going to get out of here before the cops come. Or worse."

As she walked toward him, she shrugged off her coat and shook off more glass. "Call me Annie," she said.

THE FIRST THING Garrett Skye did was tape a square of thick cardboard over the broken pane in the door and sweep up the glass. He did this work efficiently and without fanfare as Annie stood by, still shaken up and disorientated. The stream of cold the hole had allowed to enter the cabin immediately stopped and along with it, some of Annie's shivers.

Next, he produced a lethal-looking pocketknife and as Annie shrank away from the blade, cut the rope from around her wrists. As she rubbed the reddened skin, he disappeared into the kitchen, reappearing a few moments later with a small clean towel and a bowl of steaming water. He pointed at a chair and she sat down.

"I don't have a lot of time but I can't leave you here like this. I'm going to wipe the blood off your face. While I do that, you're going to talk. Your last call, made minutes before you hiked up my driveway, was to Shelby Parker. Who exactly is she?"

"You looked at my cell phone."

"Yes."

What was the use of lying? She said, "Shelby Parker is Elaine Greason's daughter."

"Elaine's daughter? The one who lives in Arizona?"

"That's the one. She got tired of waiting for the police to find you."

"So she hired *you?*"

Annie tried to look like a force to be reckoned with. "I'm sure she's called the police by now. They'll be here any minute."

"You hope," he said, dousing the cloth with water and moving it across her forehead. "Sure seems to be taking them a long time, though, doesn't it?" he added as he wrung out the cloth. The water in the bowl turned pink. Annie's stomach turned over. She wasn't good with blood, especially her own.

She cried out as he dabbed at her chin. "There's a piece of glass in there. Stay put."

He found tweezers in a cabinet and brought them back to the table, where he deftly removed the glass. "I wonder why the sheriff hasn't shown up?" he mused again as he tossed the glass chip into the waste basket.

She glanced out the big window in front. Snow. Nothing but snow. No cops running to the rescue.

He leaned back and looked at her. "I'll tell you why. The sheriff's office doesn't know my true identity because you didn't tell them. The whole town of Poplar Gulch thinks my name is Pete Jordan. They believe I'm a professor friend of Ben Miller's, using his place to recover from knee surgery. I don't talk a lot, but I'm friendly, ride Ben's horse on occasion, and pay my bills with cash."

"But—"

"Your cuts are minor." He took the bowl and cloth back to the kitchen and returned with a box of bandages and a tube of ointment which he applied with a cotton-tipped stick. The bandages went on next. One near her temple and another on her left cheek. Two over the gash on her chin.

She looked at his face as he worked. He needed a shave. The dark stubble made him look raw, sexy, male. On second thought, perhaps he didn't need a shave.

She took a steadying breath but all that accomplished was filling her nostrils with his woodsy scent. She was way too aware of him as a man, considering the fact he was a murderer. She'd read about those women who get all emotionally attached to vicious fiends and spend their life trotting back and forth to prison cells for conjugal visits. No, thanks.

"Why didn't Parker tell you to contact the police when you found me?" he said. "Why contact her?"

Because that's the way my dad organized it. She wasn't going to tell him that. Let this guy think she had connections and experience. And a husband if he wanted. The bigger, the better.

He sat on his heels and directed a flashlight into her eyes. Wasn't it obvious by now her eyes were fine?

"Don't blink," he said. "Anything hurt?"

"No." She stared into his bottomless brown orbs, intrigued by the swirls of burnt sienna until she blinked rapidly and pushed his hand away.

Had she really just sat there meekly and let him attend to her wounds, gazing into his eyes like a goof? Maybe she'd been in shock. If so, she was better now and she wanted a little elbow room. She said, "I'm good. Thanks."

He switched off the flashlight and stood. Perching on the edge of the table, he said, "If Parker wants her mother's alleged killer brought to justice, why direct her private eye to call her instead of the cops?"

"Alleged?" she said, sitting forward. "Didn't you kill Elaine Greason?"

He stared at her. "Does it matter? You don't care if I'm guilty or innocent, right? Just as long as you collect your money. You can't be a bounty hunter because I was never bonded. Why don't you have some kind of license or permit? You were carrying concealed. Is that lawful between Nevada and California?"

She ignored his questions because she didn't really know what he was talking about. Was there a law against a concerned citizen tracking down a wanted killer? Her intention had never been to confront him.

He frowned at her, narrowing those rich, dark eyes in the process.

He said, "You took that picture of me in the truck when I went to see my daughter."

She nodded as though she knew this was a fact. In truth, she had no idea when or where her father took the picture. But she did know Skye had left a little girl in Reno. In fact, that knowledge had tipped the scales in her mind when it came to looking for him. She had no patience for men who abandoned their children.

"So you know about Megan. You didn't mention her to the Parker woman, did you?"

"Why would it matter?" she said. "The cops don't want your daughter."

"If it's the cops she has in mind, no," he said.

"What do you mean?"

"Did you or didn't you mention Megan on the phone?"

"I don't remember," Annie said. Had she?

His gaze turned introspective for a second. Then he took a heavy-looking gold watch from his pocket. He'd looked at the watch in the parking lot of the store. She hadn't noticed the cover design before, but she did now. The heavy embossing depicted a bridge arcing over a river. He popped it open, checked the time and repocketed the watch.

"Why is it so important?" she asked.

He stood abruptly and walked into the kitchen. His limp was better. When he returned, he carried a length of rope.

"Oh, no, you don't," she said, standing. "You are not going to tie me up again. I refuse."

He spared her a cursory glance. "I'm going to bank the fire," he said. "It should stay warm until morning. I'd leave you free to move around the cabin, but you'd just follow me."

"What—"

He picked up the rifle from where it sat against the wall. It had been sitting there when he went to the kitchen and she hadn't grabbed it and turned it on him. Merciful heavens, she had zero survival instincts. He pointed it at her. "Don't let my friendly smile fool you, Annie. The last time I escaped I shot a man."

"Randy Larson."

"Right. And I *liked* Randy." He gestured toward the big heavy chair by the fireplace. "Sit down."

"And if I don't?"

"I'll shoot you."

"You wouldn't."

He strode toward her, any semblance of a smile gone, grim determination settling in his eyes. She scrambled back until she more or less fell into the big chair. For a second she thought of fighting him but abandoned that thought as she caught another glimpse of the rifle. He stooped over her, pinning her to the chair with the sheer volume of his body.

"It's for your own good," he said, staring down into her eyes.

"Sure it is," she said.

Setting the rifle aside, he once again tied a rope around her wrists. The knot wasn't very tight. Then he knelt and secured her ankles. He used additional knots to secure her to the chair. The effort seemed halfhearted.

He stood when he was finished. "Maybe you should find a new line of work. Something a little less violent."

"You wish," she said.

He cracked a smile. Shaking his head, he took the duffel bag into the kitchen. She heard him opening and closing drawers before reappearing. He held a bottle of water.

"It's too late to untie you and give you something to eat. I'll help you take a drink."

"So I'll have to sit here without a bathroom? Thanks anyway."

"You'll get thirsty."

"I'll live. I got away once, I can do it again."

"Suit yourself," he said as he banked the fire by adjusting the flue and closing the glass door.

Damn. The rest of Shelby Parker's money was about to saunter down the hill and there wasn't a thing she could do about it.

Annie mentally apologized to her dead father

and his living widow. Sorry about the loan sharks, sorry about being a failure, sorry, sorry, sorry.

Garrett snagged a thick jacket off a hook by the front door and shrugged it on over the leather jacket he still wore. Opening the duffel once again, he dropped in her wallet and cell phone, the camera and her father's gun.

"Wait a second," she protested. "Those things are mine."

"There's no phone in this cabin. I'll borrow yours so I can call someone to come get Scio. I didn't tie you very tight. You should be able to get out of the ropes in an hour or so. All I need is a head start."

"There's no need for ropes—"

"Sure there is. You have dollar signs in your eyes. If you're still tied up in the morning when someone comes to get Scio, try hollering."

"And the rest?"

"I'm doing you and the world a favor by disarming you."

"You're a thief as well as a killer," she said.

A smile tipped his face from handsome to roguish. He once again knelt by the chair. This time he ran his fingers along her jaw. His touch did something to her, enflamed something inside she'd kept buried. She tried to twist her head away, but couldn't and it wasn't because ropes restrained her.

"Goodbye, Anastasia Ryder," he whispered. His face came close to hers, his warm breath wafted over her skin. The next thing she knew, his lips had connected with hers. For a second she forgot where she was, who he was. Caught up in sensation, she became oblivious to reality.

The man was quite a kisser. Open mouth, warm and wet, gathering her into his passion against her will. Okay, not against her will. A dizzying pulse of sensations went straight to her head, and to her groin.

And then he was standing.

"I suggest you spend the night considering other things you could do with your life," he said softly, firelight glowing on his skin.

"Because you've been so damn successful with yours?"

"Touché." With a few backward steps he was at the door. He switched on a table lamp. "Do you want me to turn on the radio or the TV?"

"I want you to come over here and untie me, that's what I want," she said, struggling against the ropes.

"No can do," he said, grabbing the rifle again. He opened the door and stepped out into the gathering dark. The door closed quietly behind him.

Watching his retreating form through the big window, she screamed his name as he disappeared into the snow.

Chapter Three

Why hadn't Shelby Parker called the sheriff? Why wasn't the place surrounded by floodlights and barking dogs and a SWAT team?

Thirty minutes of struggling accomplished nothing but rope burns. After forty-five minutes, not only had night stolen over the hillside and flooded the house with shadows but Annie's wrists had finally slipped free of the ropes.

She quickly untied her ankles and, standing, began walking around the room trying to get the feeling back in her feet.

Despite the cold, dark night and the possibility of wildlife, she planned to walk down to the main road and hitch a ride to the sheriff's station, where she would tell anyone who would listen about Garrett Skye. They could put out an APB. He'd be in jail by morning. He could try sweet-talking the deputies. Try kissing one of them. See how far it got him.

And then she was going to call Shelby Parker and demand the rest of her father's money. After all, Skye's location had been verified. It wasn't her fault he got away.

Okay, it was her fault.

After that, she was going back to her quiet life and the little kids and polite parents who made up ninety-nine percent of the people she came into contact with. And judging from the flood of sexual energy Garrett Skye's kiss had provoked, it was also time to find a new boyfriend.

Trouble was, she wasn't good with men. Two boyfriends before, she'd had a fling with a divorced man who, as it turned out, wasn't actually divorced, a revelation that had left her spoiled for men for a good year. The last boyfriend had had a gambling addiction he hid very well until Annie discovered him using her ATM card without permission.

And now an attraction to a felon. What was wrong with her?

What she needed to find was a nice man, not a dangerous one. Not a man who blew up women, not a man whose destiny seemed to be on a collision course with a life sentence in Nevada State Prison.

After a fruitless search for something sugary to eat, she settled on cold leftover spaghetti and meatballs out of Skye's refrigerator. Then she searched the cabin for a warm coat. Hers was outside and covered with glass. As a bonus, she also found insulated gloves that almost fit. She took another big knife out of the kitchen drawer. Maybe there were coyotes out there. Maybe even more dangerous beasts roamed the hillside, the two-legged variety.

One more search to find a flashlight and new batteries, strap her small purse across her chest under her coat and she was ready to go. She opened the door. Cold wind slapped her in the face. Looking out at the two inches of new snow covering the rocky, unpredictable hillside and her determination drained. Her flashlight and warm coat were no match for that miserable driveway. She'd have to think of something else.

The horse. She'd take Scio. This time she'd have time to saddle him properly and talk to him in a soothing voice. He wouldn't be afraid of her this time.

It had stopped snowing but only the faintest of moonlight made its way through the heavy cloud cover. Picking her way carefully, she made her way to the barn.

Scio wasn't in his stall. He wasn't in any of the stalls. Apparently, Garrett had taken him, which meant he wasn't going to call someone to come get the horse. What if she hadn't been able to get out of the ropes? How long would she have had to stay tied to that chair before someone came looking for her?

Another thought, even more uncomfortable. Why did it come as a surprise that Garrett Skye was untrustworthy? What in the world had she expected from a man like him?

She'd barely had a moment to consider her next move when she heard the sound of a motor. She ran to the barn door in time to see headlights sweep the tops of the trees.

At last! Shelby Parker must have finally retrieved her voice mail and called the sheriff. A car stopped on the other side of the wrecked vehicles still plugging the top of the driveway. Though giddy with relief, Annie waited for a moment to see who emerged from around the wreck. She wasn't about to get herself into another out-of-the-frying-pan-into-the-fire scenario.

Car doors closed. The silhouette of two men backlit by headlights circled the wreck and met again on Annie's side. She lifted a foot to step outside the barn.

And then one of them spoke. It wasn't his words that halted her forward progress, it was the hushed, guttural sound of his voice.

"Looks like Skye had an accident."

"Maybe he already bought the farm."

A flashlight briefly flicked over the wreckage and then went out. "I don't see a body, but the car has Nevada plates. I wonder where Ryder's daughter is?"

"She's no match for Skye," the other said. "By now she's probably dead and buried under a bush."

Both of them chuckled.

Annie's feet froze to the ground. Their chuckles were dry and sarcastic and cut through her like a polar wind. Plus, they knew about her. That meant they knew Shelby Parker, as Annie had told no one else she was coming here. But why weren't they also looking for her dad? She'd tried to make her message sound like he was with her.

"Go around back, I'll take the front," one of the men said. "Remember, don't shoot to kill, we want Skye alive."

"What if the girl shows up?"

"If she gets in the way—"

Annie's feet did an instant thaw as she shrank back inside the barn. Those men were not with the sheriff's department. What in the world was going on?

She watched from her hidden position as one man slunk past her, stray shafts of moonlight clearly revealing the gun held down by his leg. Unsure what to do next, she all but stopped breathing.

Should she risk leaving the barn?

She couldn't bring herself to step out into the open so she moved farther into the barn instead. All bravado abandoned her. What she wanted to do was find a dark corner and hunker down like a scared child. She should try to make a run for it. But the night sky was fickle, overcast one minute, moonlit the next. She kept seeing that gun and could almost feel the burning trail of a bullet piercing her spine, the sudden lack of feeling in her legs....

Thank heavens she wasn't still tied up in the house.

She moved deeper inside until she backed into a ladder and then she climbed. The ladder emptied into the loft with an open hay door through which moonlight shone. The loft was full of straw and what looked like old tarps. She knew she couldn't use the flashlight. Was the straw deep enough to burrow into? Wait, she had a kitchen knife. She could stab someone.

Before the other one shot her dead?

Caught in an agony of indecision, she approached the hay door, able to see only the night sky from her vantage point. The scene outside looked so peaceful. The moon high, clouds drifting in front of it, snow glittering on the tops of tree boughs.

There was a part of her that felt sure she could

explain herself to those two men and hitch a ride out of here once they found Garrett had already left. There was a part of her that wanted this interminable day to be over, that couldn't quite believe these men were the murderers they sounded like.

They move as though they've slithered through the dark a hundred times before. Use your head, Annie.

The voices, when they came again, sounded even closer. She moved toward the edge of the hay door in able to scan the ground. One of the men stood in the open doorway of the cabin, the other stood on the front porch. The cabin light illuminated them both. One was a huge, bald brute, the other shorter with straight dark hair and a twist to his mouth that seemed more sneer than smile. They both wore overcoats and polished shoes and looked as though they'd just stepped off a city sidewalk.

"He's not in here," the bald man said from the cabin door. "He hasn't been gone long, though. The fire's still burning in the stove."

A moment of silence, followed by, "Torch the house. That should cover our bases. I'll check the barn."

Annie ran to the ladder. She had to escape the barn right now. If they planned to burn down the house, the barn might be next. Her foot had touched the second rung when she heard one of them holler, "Skye? If you're in there come on out. There's no use hiding." He stepped inside the barn, gun held out in front.

Had he heard her? She stood perfectly still, hoping the shadows hid her foot on the ladder.

"He's not in the barn," the man said, his voice softer as though he had turned away to speak.

The other thug moved into view. Thanks to the flaming piece of wood he held in one hand, Annie could see the top of his dark head through the open spaces on the ladder. Apparently he'd taken care of his arson job and brought the means to start another fire. As they continued talking, Annie slowly raised her bottom foot and shifted her weight on the ladder.

And once again fought the desire to announce herself and take her chances.

"Looks like he got away."

"Burn this place down, too. It's unlikely he left it, but you never know. Time we start back to Reno."

"Without Skye? And what about the girl? There'll be trouble—"

"We'll stake out the Reno place tomorrow. We'd better get out of here before someone calls the fire department."

Annie glanced to the hay door which now glowed with light given off by the flaming house next door. She glanced back at the men who both turned and walked out of the barn, one of them still carrying the makeshift torch. Maybe the plan was to let the house fire catch the barn. At the last moment, the flaming wood came sailing back into the barn where it landed against the new bales of hay Garrett had bought that morning. The bales instantly caught fire. Annie raced across the loft.

The men had stopped to look at the car/truck wreck at the top of the drive and she caught herself just in time at the hay door. "Go away," she muttered, willing them with her desperation to get in their car and drive off before the fire caught the straw in the loft.

And as if hearing her, they threw one last look toward the cabin and barn, then circled the wreck and got in their car. Annie barely heard the slam of doors and the revving of the engine over the increasingly loud roar of the fire.

She raced back to the ladder to find it engulfed. She'd have to jump which would mean a broken leg. Could she crawl to safety with a broken leg? No. She couldn't jump twenty feet. She needed a rope. She could shimmy down a rope. She had gloves to protect her hands. She began tossing hay, looking for a piece of rope while knowing it was unlikely one would be hidden under loose hay or old tarps. She'd lost the knife somewhere.

Smoke rose in the barn faster than the flames and she doubled over, coughing.

"Annie!"

She straightened up, listening.

The voice came again, louder this time. "Annie! Where are you?"

She ran across the loft to the hay door, shielding her face with her arm. "Up here!" she yelled. Was that Garrett's voice? But he'd been gone so long....

"I see you," he yelled.

Annie peered through the smoke. She finally made out a big bay horse and the man astride it. Her heart rate quadrupled as adrenaline pumped through her body.

"Jump," Garrett called.

Jump? What, like the Lone Ranger from the top of a giant rock onto the willing back of his noble steed, Silver?

What's your option? Jump now as a human being, wait another moment and jump as a shish kebab.

"Here I come," she screamed, and taking a few steps back, dashed for the hay door and sailed into the night like a kid plunging into a cool lake on the hottest day of summer.

KEEPING SCIO CLOSE to the burning barn took all Garrett's concentration. The horse was terrified of the flames and smoke and who could blame him?

Where was Annie? Why didn't she jump?

He heard her yell something and looked up in

time to see her flying through the night air, almost in slow motion, until she landed in his arms and Scio, as though sensing it was okay now to do what common sense had been urging him to do from the beginning, took off down the hill.

It was tense going for a few moments as the horse gave in to his panic, the woman slipped forward on the horse's neck and Garrett fought to keep one hand on her and the other on the reins. It was dark down among the trees and the footing was uneven. He couldn't see where they were going and was left to trust the horse's ability to avoid trees and ditches.

They reached the bottom of the hill in record time. As the land flattened out, the horse began to slow down. Eventually, Garrett was able to pull Annie closer to his chest and wrap an arm around her waist. The awful feeling she was about to slip from his grasp to be trampled underfoot lessened. She held on to the saddle horn, though he saw during flashes of moonlight that she'd also grabbed a healthy handful of Scio's mane and twisted it through her fingers.

He regained control of the horse before the highway. As the sound of thundering hoofbeats retreated, another noise filled the night air: sirens, in the distance, on their way. He looked through the trees, straining for a glimpse of the top of the mountain. A few feet farther on, they'd cleared all the trees and he was able to reign Scio in. They both turned in the saddle to look back.

The burning house and barn crowned the hill as Ben Miller's cabin and barn went up in smoke. An explosion followed by high flames announced the fire had spread to the car and the truck. The only thing to be thankful for was that rescue equipment was on the way and the fire wouldn't engulf the whole hill.

He heard Annie groan. "Are you okay?"

She turned even farther until they were nose to nose. All he could see was the twinkle of ambient light reflected in her eyes. She smelled strongly of smoke.

"Am I okay?" she repeated. "I am so *not* okay it's not funny." And with that she turned back around and started coughing.

Once she'd stopped, he said, "What happened back there?"

"A couple of guys came to see you. They were annoyed you weren't home so they burned down your house."

"Shelby Parker's men?"

"I think so. They knew about me."

"The police—"

"Trust me, they didn't call the police."

He got off the horse, caught Annie as she slid

to the ground, got back in the saddle and, lowering a hand, grabbed her arm and helped her swing up behind him. She tucked her hips as close to his as possible and wrapped her arms around him. As they continued on, her head rested against his back though her grip on his torso never loosened.

Scio's hot breath created a cloud of vapor in the moonlight as his hoofs cracked through the icy snow. Garrett admitted to himself it felt good to have Annie plastered against his back. Too good. To ward off increasingly erotic thoughts, he concentrated on what he should do next.

The first thing was easy—get as far away from the hill as possible. But the horse had had a traumatic time of it and was now carrying two adults. Garrett didn't dare ask Scio to do more than amble along.

Keeping off the road, they rode for another mile. As they were riding away from town, the sounds of sirens grew fainter. Garrett could think of only one place to go and that was Joanna's. He could leave Scio with her and from there, Annie Ryder could call her husband for a ride back to Reno.

And he could disappear.

Never to see Megan again? He couldn't bear to think about his little girl so he put her out of his mind.

Other than a few strings of twinkling Christmas

lights around the windows, Joanna's house was dark. The barn was dimly lit, however. He paused by the big bell she kept on a post outside her house and rang it. When no answering lights went on in the house, he gathered she was gone for the evening and allowed Scio to head for the barn.

Joanna's horses greeted them with whinnies and curious tosses of their heads as they peered out of their stalls. Garrett rode to the center unsaddling area. He helped Annie dismount before getting off the horse himself. Annie stood right next to him for a moment, knees shaking, though whether it was from riding, fear or injury, he didn't know.

"Are you hurt?" he asked her, thinking he needed to turn on brighter lights and make sure she wasn't bleeding anywhere.

She looked up at him, eyes blazing, bandages still stuck to her sooty face in a trio of places. He expected a slap or a tirade or something equally hostile. Instead, she stood on her tiptoes, put both arms around his neck and pulled his head down closer to hers.

"Thank you for coming back for me. You saved my life," she said, and with that, planted her lips on his. The wild kiss that followed chased away the fire and the night.

She was soft, she was feminine, she was small

and she was fierce. When her tongue touched his, his hands slipped down to cup her rear. He almost lifted her off her feet.

Maybe it was what they'd been through together that day, maybe it was the odd circumstances of their getaway, maybe it was the fear of loss and the joy of not being dead. Whatever it was, he was ready to make good on that kiss and tote her off into the hay. Except…

He clasped both her wrists and pulled away. "Wait a second," he said. "You're married."

"That didn't seem to faze you earlier tonight," she said with a few warm kisses against his throat.

"Earlier tonight I was never going to see you again."

"I'm not married," she said.

"But the car is registered to Jack Ryder."

"My father. Recently deceased."

"I'm sorry."

She said, "You shouldn't be. If he hadn't died, you'd be riding back to Reno with two thugs, names unknown."

He had no idea what her remark meant, but the wistful smile following it piqued his interest. He'd known she was pretty from the moment the bad wig slipped off her head, but standing here in the half light, her coppery hair shimmering, cheeks flushed, peachy lips curved just the tiniest bit, she looked breathtaking. Despite the smoke. Despite the bandages.

Once again he considered his options.

"Who's Joanna?" she said.

"I need to hear about the thugs," he answered, returning to the business at hand. There was no time for impulsive lovemaking with a stranger hired to get him. What was he thinking?

"Why did you come back for me?"

That question was a hard one to answer and best delayed. He said, "Joanna owns this place. She boards Scio for Ben Miller during the winter. Speaking of Scio, he's had a hard night."

"So have I," she said, stepping back.

He released his grip on her delicate wrists.

"Why did you come back?" she asked again, head tilted, hair falling softly around her heart-shaped face, eyes inquisitive.

He thought for a moment, then walked away.

Chapter Four

"You said there were two thugs," Garrett said an hour later.

They'd taken his duffel into the tack room and hunkered down to talk. They had a few granola bars, bottled water, a couple of apples he'd packed at the cabin, plus her cell phone, camera and her dad's gun.

They'd rubbed down Scio after his walk. The big bay gelding, now locked into a stall, munched on hay, a blanket secured on his back. He looked cleaner, drier, and better fed than either one of them.

Annie stretched out her legs and took a bite of a Golden Delicious. Though the stall was plush by barn standards, it was still drafty and cold. What she wouldn't give for a shower and realized with a start that she still had a room at the motel in Poplar Gulch. That meant clean clothes!

"Annie?"

"Sorry. Okay, two men drove up. They cracked a few jokes about the wreck at the top of the driveway then went looking for you. They said you'd probably killed me and buried me on the hill. And then they laughed." It still made her tremble deep inside.

"What did they look like?"

Annie described them: one bald, one a smiling man with a single eyebrow.

"Sounds like they were distinctive," Garrett said.

"Do you know them?"

"No. Did they know about you? Did they know your name?"

"Yes."

"Did anyone besides Shelby Parker know you intended to come to Ben Miller's cabin?"

"Nope, and that means they know Shelby Parker, right? That means Shelby sent them instead of the police. Why?"

"I don't know. I expected Klugg to try something like this, but what does Shelby Parker want with me?"

"Well, you did kill her mother."

As soon as the words left her lips, Annie had one reaction followed by another. The first was a jolt of pure panic: she was munching on an apple while in the company of a killer.

The second reaction was just as strong. *No, she wasn't.* This man wasn't a killer, at least not in the cold-blooded way Annie suspected the two gangster-types who had burned down Ben Miller's cabin might be.

"I didn't kill her mother," he said. "But I guess Shelby doesn't know that. What I mean is why doesn't she want me brought to justice? Why would she want me brought to her? To kill me herself? Isn't that a little far-fetched? And wouldn't she be concerned about your safety?"

"Beats me. Maybe someone tapped Shelby's phone, maybe they heard she hired my father and were waiting to get a message that he'd found you."

"I wouldn't put anything past Klugg."

"But they never mentioned the name Klugg, you know."

He rubbed his temples.

"Who is this guy, anyway?"

"Klugg?" He finished off a granola bar, and brushed the crumbs from his fingers. "He used to be a boxer. He owns a string of health clubs now as well as a few gyms where people train. When two of his associates ended up dead, he was charged with hiring a hit man. Elaine was his attorney. He blamed her when he got a guilty conviction. First he fired her and then he started making threats."

"What kind of threats?"

"The kind that make a person scared to go out in the dark. Someone followed her home one night, ramming her bumper, turning off their headlights and then there was a delivery of dead roses—stuff like that."

"But you said Klugg was in jail."

"Trust me, a guy like Klugg maintains connections on the outside. All he has to do is give orders."

"Why would anyone think you'd kill Elaine Greason? What motive would you have had?"

He was silent for a moment, then took a deep breath. "I went to see Klugg in prison."

"Then you know him?" She couldn't keep the shock out of her voice.

"No, I don't know him. What happened was this—he demanded a visit from Elaine. She didn't want anything more to do with him. I was supposed to tell Klugg to leave Elaine alone or she'd get a court order. I delivered the message. The man stared at me like I was a piece of dead meat. The cops decided that meeting was when Klugg hired me to take care of Elaine for him."

"Then the motive they settled on was—"

"Money. I heard they found an envelope of unexplained cash in my apartment after I left. It appeared I had motive, opportunity and the know-how because I worked briefly with munitions in the army. I was like the poster boy for this murder. Add to that the fact I got into a gunfight with

Randy Larson when he tried to detain me, and it doesn't look so good."

"No," she said, "it doesn't. If you didn't kill Elaine Greason and Klugg did then he's going to want your mouth permanently closed."

"Exactly," he said.

For Annie, the euphoria of escaping the fire was being quickly replaced by anxiety. What was she doing in a world of murder and arson and assassins? She was a preschool teacher!

She thought back to hiding in the barn, to lurking in the hay loft, and suppressed a shudder.

"Tell me what else those men said."

"It sounded as though they were ready to shoot me if they saw me."

"I'm sorry I left you tied up," he said. "It's a good thing you're such a pro at getting free."

"Why would Shelby agree to that? What have I ever done to her?" *Besides lie about my father's condition,* Annie added to herself. But no one was supposed to know about that.

"You're apparently the only one who knows she's out to get rid of me," Garrett said. "But again, if Klugg is intercepting her messages, she may not even have gotten the one you left. It might have gone directly to him. When you met with her, did she say anything to suggest she wasn't acting alone?"

Since Annie had never actually spoken with the woman, she shook her head. She got up and walked over to Scio, offering him the rest of her apple, glad to be out from under Garrett's scrutiny for a second.

The big horse daintily sniffed the apple before nibbling from it with huge teeth. Annie handed it over, glad to escape with all her fingers.

"Did those goons say what they were going to do next?" Garrett said.

She turned to face him, standing with her back to Scio's stall. She tried hard not to think about the many times she'd avoided death that night, but the harrowing memories were stacking up like planes over a busy airport. "When they decided to burn the house and barn," she said, "I got the feeling it was to get rid of something. Not someone, something. Oh, and they said they would try the Reno place tomorrow. They said they would stake it out."

Garrett grew very still. "The Reno place?"

"What does it mean?" she asked, stepping closer.

"The only place I had in Reno was an apartment at the back of Greason's property. Even if it was still mine, they wouldn't go there."

"But it's not yours anymore?"

"Of course not. A man doesn't pay the rent for a man he believes blew up his loving wife."

"I guess not."

"Plus, he saw me shoot poor Randy. Trust me, Greason isn't losing sleep worrying about keeping a roof over my head. And if two goons show up and he figures they're in any way connected to his wife's murder, he'll have the cops there so fast…"

"How about your daughter? She lives in Reno."

"But they don't know her name. My ex took her maiden name back and I didn't advertise Megan's existence."

"Did you tell Elaine or her husband about Megan? Might they have mentioned her to Elaine's daughter?"

"They both knew about Megan, of course. I doubt I ever mentioned her last name, though."

"Maybe I mentioned Megan on that damn phone message to Shelby Parker and if it's true they're intercepting her messages—"

"But you said you didn't."

"I said I couldn't remember," she corrected.

"Think, Annie."

Events had been racing along at such a pace that Annie hadn't really concentrated on what she'd told Shelby Parker before this. She bit her lip and took a few steps back and forth. "I told Ms. Parker you were in Poplar Gulch. I mentioned the name Ben Miller because I'd seen it on the mailbox and remembered it from your file."

"My file?"

"Well—"

"Never mind, that's how the thugs knew where to come look for me. Did you tell Parker how you happened to know about Poplar Gulch in the first place? About the picture of me in Ben's truck taken outside my ex-wife's house?"

Annie stopped pacing as her heart dropped to her feet. She faced Garrett. "Oh, my gosh, I did say just about exactly that. But I didn't say her name."

"Still, they know I have a daughter and an ex-wife."

"If I've hurt your little girl because I was too stupid to remember this before, I'll never forgive myself. I'm so sorry—"

Garrett reached for the cell phone. As he waited for it to power up, indecision stole over his face.

"What is it?" Annie asked, sitting down beside him again.

"I don't know who to call." He took out his pocket watch and checked the time. "It's almost midnight."

"I forgot your ex-wife is a dancer at one of the casinos. She'll be at work."

He looked up with alarm. "What else do you know about me?"

"Mother dead, father and brother in Oregon, infant nephew—"

"What? Infant nephew? Brady has a kid?"

"Named Nathan. And a wife. Former name Lara Kirk."

"Lara Kirk? As in the Riverport Kirk family?"

"I don't know about that."

"I wonder what else I missed."

"Call Megan's grandmother," Annie said.

"You know about my ex-wife's mother, too?"

"She's a semi-invalid and watches Megan while your ex goes to work. Call her."

"If I told her to take Megan away from Reno right now, she'd hang up on me."

"Then call the police."

"And tell them what?" He ran a hand through his thick, dark hair. "I'm a wanted man," he said softly. "If Megan disappears into the system I'll never get her back. But I can't go to Reno—"

"Why not?"

"It might lead them to her."

"But she needs you. I mean, apart from the fact she hasn't seen you in months and to a little kid that's a lifetime, there may be two really awful men on their way to her house. She needs you to protect her."

He stared at the phone without answering.

Annie got to her feet. "What are you waiting for?"

"Listen here—"

"Are you going to leave your little girl to fend for herself until you get your life all straightened out?"

He glared at her a few more moments before saying, "If I don't show up, Megan will be okay. The thugs will decide I've skipped and leave her alone. Once I show up, she'll be in horrible danger. Just like you were tonight."

"You're walking away from your own daughter."

"I don't have a choice. It's why I left Reno in the first place. Megan is safer without me hanging around. They may not even know she's living under her mother's name."

"But they might. If my—if I can figure it out, so can they. How can you say she's safer without her father? How can you be so selfish?"

She suddenly noticed he was standing, too. He took a step toward her, eyes murderous. "You don't know what you're talking about."

"Yes, I do," she all but growled, her voice growing distressingly thick with emotion as her own past reared its ugly head in her mind. She took a deep breath. "I absolutely do know what I'm talking about. A little girl needs her father, no matter what. This isn't just about you, it's about her, too. Her mother stays out most nights and her grandmother resents babysitting and lives on painkillers, and her father is hiding—"

"How do you know all this? No, don't tell me. You must be better at your job than I gave you credit for."

"Megan needs you and you're running away. Again."

He stomped off a few feet toward Scio's stall and stood staring at the horse, hands shoved in his coat pockets. Annie picked up the phone he'd left sitting on the hay. Maybe she could call a taxi to come get her. She'd have to wait until her fingers stopped trembling.

Garrett returned. He scooped up his duffel bag, took out a pencil and a piece of paper and started writing.

"What are you doing?"

He said, "Making a note for Joanna. Explaining there was a fire at Ben's place, telling her I'm leaving. She boards Ben's horse during the winter. I only had him for a few weeks."

"Where are you going?" she asked as she saw him sign the name Pete Jordan to the note.

"To Reno."

"How?"

"I'll borrow Joanna's hay truck. She keeps an extra key in a grain bag." He scribbled something about taking the truck on the bottom of the note before sticking it through a nail located next to Scio's stall.

Annie bit her lip. God help her, and him, and little Megan, if she was wrong about this. Who was she to stand there and tell him what to do? What if he was right? What if his going back to Reno proved to be the absolutely wrong thing to do?

"Listen," she said, feeling foolish and too young to be let out alone. "Maybe you shouldn't listen to me, Garrett. Maybe you're right about this whole thing and I'm wrong."

He lifted her chin with his finger and, leaning down, kissed her. The touch of his lips wrapped her in anxiety.

A second later, he walked away, his limp barely noticeable.

Annie jumped to her feet again. "I'm going with you."

"No, you're not," he called over his shoulder.

"Why not?"

"It's dangerous."

She laughed. "Like the whole night hasn't been dangerous? Remember me, almost a human torch?"

He paused midstep and turned. Gone was the amiable, handsome man with whom she'd spent a few blissful moments. His dark eyes were black as he said, "Not now, Annie." He turned and strode off.

Well, she was on a mission, too. She took her father's gun out of her bag. She hadn't told Garrett she wasn't a private detective though it appeared he assumed it. But she hadn't told him. She leveled the gun and cocked it. The click sounded like thunder in the quiet barn. Garrett heard it and turned around again, his expression more annoyed than worried.

"I'm going with you," she said, pointing the gun at his heart, holding it with both hands. He opened his mouth so she spoke quickly. "I need to get back to Reno and I have no car. Until I'm positive I can't turn you in for the other half of my twenty-thousand-dollar fee, I'm not letting you out of my sight."

"Twenty thousand? Didn't that strike you as an awful lot of money? Didn't you suspect something fishy was going on? What kind of detective are you?"

"I found you, didn't I?"

"I have to assume that was an accident," he said. His voice still dripping with sarcasm, he added, "So, now you're going to shoot me?"

"Just in the foot."

"Did you put bullets in the gun?"

She said, "Of course I did."

"No, you didn't. There hasn't been time. You're in the wrong line of work."

She lowered the gun.

He stared at her a heartbeat longer before saying, "What the hell. Okay, come on, you might as well ride with me."

"I want to know why you came back tonight," she said, stuffing the empty gun back in her bag.

"That's a damn good question," he said and added with a glint in his eyes, "Everybody makes mistakes."

Chapter Five

They drove into Poplar Gulch, where Garrett insisted Annie take the time to let herself into room seven of the Shut Eye Inn and pack her belongings. After throwing her suitcase in the hay truck, she went into the office and settled her bill. It occurred to him as he watched her through the glass window that she could easily be turning him in, the cops could show up any second, she might still be hoping to salvage the rest of her fee. He was almost surprised when she came back to the truck and climbed inside.

She was either very trusting or very naive.

Looking at him, she said, "Why did we waste twenty minutes with all this?"

"No reason to alert the cops they had a missing woman in town whose last name matched the registration on what's left of your dad's car up in Ben's driveway. If anyone ever bothers to check."

He'd been worried about leaving his fingerprints all over the truck and cabin. This was no longer a concern as everything had since gone up in smoke. He happened to know Ben hadn't insured the cabin as he'd had plans to tear it down the coming spring and build himself a new summerhouse. With any luck, the mess on the top of the hill would be a nonissue at least until Garrett took Megan far away where they could start over.

"Good thinking," Annie said.

After leaving town, they drove in silence for several miles. Garrett was too wound up to engage in chitchat. He kept expecting to see red lights in the rearview mirror. He kept picturing two thugs walking up to his ex-mother-in-law's door and swiping Megan.

It was hard to swallow the panic that swelled in his throat. Sitting in the seat beside him, Annie was just as quiet though why was anyone's guess.

Frankly, he wasn't sure what to make of her. She wasn't like the other women he'd been attracted to in the past. She didn't look like them or move like them or react like them.

Face it, the Annies of the world had always been a mystery to him. The Annies of the world had never given him a second glance. It was like they sensed the drifting troublemaker in him and steered clear.

But not this Annie.

The best thing he could do for both of them was

get rid of her. He said, "If we get pulled over by the cops, I'm going to hold your gun on you. Don't tell them anything about helping me."

"Have I helped you?" she said.

"Come to think of it, no, not really."

"Then it'll be easy."

After a few additional miles, she stirred in her seat as though trying to make up her mind about something. He kept his eyes on the dark stretch of deserted highway ahead and waited her out.

"I'm not a private detective," she said at last.

He'd already figured this out. He said, "How do you know so much about me?"

"My father was the private eye. He collected the information."

"You said he died recently."

"Yes. A heart attack."

"So, Shelby Parker hired him?"

"Yes. That's why I don't know why Parker asked my father to notify her instead of the police when he found you. And that's why I've made one stupid mistake after another."

"What are you when you're not sleuthing?" he asked.

"I work at the Desert Oasis Preschool. My specialty is prekindergarten. I also like to bake. Mostly cookies."

He laughed. One quick glance her way informed

him she didn't appreciate his reaction, but it struck him as funny. He eventually stopped chuckling, checked the rearview mirror and said, "Why in the world did you take over your father's job?"

"In three words? Vivian Beaumont Ryder."

"I've never heard of her."

Annie waited a second before saying, "No reason why you should have. She's my stepmother."

"And you and she are real friendly?"

"No, actually, I've only met her once. I wasn't exactly close to my father. In fact, up until the day he died, I'd only seen him three times since my fifth birthday. And Vivian was his sixth wife."

"You're losing me," he said.

"Dad liked women. Lots of women."

As that character assessment struck a little too close to home for comfort, Garrett asked another question. "Why are you helping a woman you don't know well? You took on a job that brought you face-to-face with danger. That seems a little over the top to me."

"Me, too," Annie said, frowning.

He thought about Randy for a moment. He'd had to defend himself when Randy pulled a gun, but it still rankled him. Big, goofy Randy was just a kid paying the bills while training for his dream of becoming a pro wrestler. Had Garrett's bullet wiped out that dream?

Annie crossed her legs and settled back in the seat as though preparing herself to tell a long story. Fine by him. Conversation might keep him from worrying himself to death.

"Dad came to see me six days ago," she said.

Megan's birthday was six days ago. He'd been parked outside his ex's house, waiting for a glimpse of his baby. It was spooky to think someone else had been watching him.

"Dad wanted to take me to dinner. He said he was leaving town the next day, that he was on a job but the road out of town was plugged. He said it didn't matter, he knew where his man was going." She paused for a second and then added, "He was talking about you."

"Yeah. There was a horrible accident that day."

"I know. I read about it in the paper the next morning."

"So, you went to dinner with your father," he prompted.

"No. Actually, I…I didn't."

That surprised him. He spared her another look. "Why?"

He thought she might have shrugged. At last she said, "I didn't go because I was angry he thought he could use me to fill a few idle hours. The truth is I'd spent my whole life wishing he wanted me and when he tried to get friendly, I turned him away because I'd decided it was too late. He died later that night."

"Guilt," Garrett said succinctly. He knew about guilt. All about it. Guilt for leaving his brother, Brady, to care for their father, guilt for leaving Elaine's car unattended, guilt for running out on Megan.

"A day later," Annie continued, "Vivian showed up. She said she wasn't telling anyone else Dad was dead. She pleaded with me to take up where my father had left off."

"Why?"

"Shelby Parker had paid my dad a retainer, half of the money up front. He'd promptly gambled it away. Trouble was, he apparently also gambled away the second half, the half he hadn't made yet. Somehow, the loan shark, a guy named Mox, found out about Dad's death. Mox told Vivian she had two weeks to pay up or she was toast."

"Mox? Man, he's a mean SOB. I ran into him a few times at the casino where I worked security before I became a bodyguard. Your stepmother is wise to take his threats seriously."

Annie laughed softly. "You do realize the reason she wants me to turn you over to Shelby Parker is to get the money to pay off Mox, don't you?"

"Makes for a certain conflict of interest," he said.

"You're right about the guilt. I feel terrible

about turning away my father. I guess he tried and all it did was irritate the daylights out of me."

"You didn't know he'd die that night, Annie."

"I know, but I still feel bad. I think I decided to help Vivian out as a sort of atonement for rejecting my dad. Plus, she's not really so bad. Just kind of—ineffectual. The thought of someone breaking one of her legs makes me sick."

Garrett thought the woman would be lucky if all Mox did was break one of her legs but he didn't say so.

Annie sighed as she added, "Are you close to your father?"

He laughed, but not like before, not with mirth, just with the absurdity of the question. He said, "My father is an alcoholic. The only one he's close to is Jim Beam."

"How about your mother? She died in a car crash, right?"

"Yeah, she'd been drinking."

"Both of them drinkers? That must have been hard."

"I think it was harder on my brother. Brady isn't that much older than I am, but it kind of fell to him to take care of me. He tried his best to make our family appear normal. But, of course, it wasn't."

"I'm sorry."

He flashed her a wistful smile. "Looks like we both struck out when it comes to fathers."

"Does your brother know where you are now?"

"No. Last time I spoke to Brady was almost four months ago, back in August, just a few days before everything fell apart. He's in law enforcement. I decided not to tempt fate by contacting him again."

"So he doesn't know you're okay?"

"Define 'okay.'"

"You know what I mean. He must have heard the news reports. He must know you fled after shooting Randy Larson. He must be wondering what happened to you. I mean, it must look to him as though you dropped off the face of the earth."

"Probably."

"He must be worried."

"I doubt it. It's been years since we've seen each other."

"Then you should—"

"Annie? Will you please stop trying to fix all my family relations? It seems to me as though you have enough trouble with your own."

"But—"

"I'm not going anywhere near Brady until I can face him like a man and not a coward. He's better off wondering what happened to me than knowing about all this."

"But—"

"Please, just give it a rest."

She turned her head away from him and stared out her window. He wasn't sure if he'd offended her and at the moment he didn't particularly care. Thinking about his father and Brady made him uneasy, made him realize how thoroughly he'd screwed up. And now his actions were going to impact Megan.

Be honest, his actions had already impacted her. He'd married a woman who'd been damn near suicidal when she learned she was pregnant. A woman who now wanted to marry again. She'd contacted Garrett way before all this happened. She'd told him he could have sole custody of Megan if he forked over twenty thousand in cash. She and the new guy, Gary, that was his name, wanted to relocate to Vegas. Garrett guessed Gary didn't want another man's three-year-old daughter horning in on his honeymoon.

So, where did a guy working as a security officer at a casino get that kind of money? Enter Robert Greason. Greason was looking for a body-guard for his brilliant, beautiful wife. Brady had applied for the job. Greason had offered free room and board plus more money than he made at the casino. Garrett had jumped at it.

And two months later, Elaine Greason was dead and he was wanted for her murder.

The big question now was this: if he wasn't there to pay off his ex and take care of Megan, who would? What would happen to her?

"I'm sorry," he said after another twenty miles of tortured memories and useless speculation. If he had to drive all the way back to Reno with his own thoughts for company, hell, he might as well stop beside the road and shoot himself now. "Come on, Annie, I'm sorry."

She still didn't answer.

They passed through a small town closed up tighter than a drum and he glanced at the fuel gauge. Almost empty, but the lone gas station was as dark as every other building.

"Annie?"

The road led out of town, down a straight stretch. He glanced at her again, but all he could see was the back of her head, a tumble of rich-auburn hair on her shoulders and her hand resting on her thigh. The relaxed pose of her fingers told him why she hadn't responded.

She was asleep.

And just like that, fatigue marched right in and set up camp behind his eyes. His aching leg joined the party a second later. It took him a couple of miles to find a wide spot off the road where it would be safe to pull over for was left of the night, though the thought of stopping frustrated the hell out of him. He couldn't keep his eyes open another minute, though, and the little light on the fuel gauge had just blinked on.

Annie didn't stir. He took off his seat belt and leaned back against his door, knowing the cold would wake one or both of them up before long.

Megan's sweet face appeared before his closed eyes and all of a sudden, the months he'd spent hiding revealed themselves for what they really were—wasted months of Megan's young life. Months he would never get back. He should have taken his chances with the law, he should never have left Reno.

He should never have left his little girl.

But then, what choice had he had? He couldn't be a father if he was in jail and he couldn't be a father if he was hiding away from his child.

He closed his eyes. There was only one solution. Get Megan away from Reno and start over somewhere else.

Run. But this time, take Megan with him.

ANNIE AWOKE with her cheek plastered against the cold glass. It was barely light outside but she could tell they were in the middle of nowhere. The sun was just barely tipping over the top of distant hills.

She raised her head, surprised when a pain in her neck made her wince. Maybe it was the result of the way she'd slept, maybe it was due to the car crash the day before. Rubbing her neck, she looked across the seat as a string of cars went by, their headlights illuminating Garrett's face. He was out like a light.

He was also twice as good-looking as she remembered from the day before. The dark stubble of yesterday was thicker now and covered the lower half of his face, his lashes lay on his cheekbones, his hair fell forward onto his forehead, brushing the tops of his brows.

She got out of the truck quietly and walked out onto the plain, stumbling over a few rocks, snagging her jeans on some thorny weeds. Her breath vaporized and she shivered. As she turned to walk back to the truck, a semi streaked by on the nearby highway and backlit Garrett walking toward her, his gait a little stiff.

She wrapped her hands around her arms, trying to warm herself. It wasn't snowy here, but a thin cold wind cut through her clothes.

"Morning," he said. She could see the general shape of his face, the glittering of his eyes, the dark bulk of his body. "I'd like to get going," he added.

"Sure."

"We'll have to retrace our tracks to the little town a mile or two back. We're out of gas."

"Maybe they'll have coffee," she said. "Lots of it."

The gas station did have coffee, as well as fresh donuts. After washing most of the soot off her face in the restroom, Annie bought a supply of both. The sun finished rising while Garrett pumped gas.

How was he going to pay for it? If he left Reno in such a hurry, what had he been living on? She got out of the truck and offered to help with the gas.

"No need," he said, smiling down at her. His eyes, so dark and intense, drew her in as they always did, doing away with her peripheral vision. She kind of melted a little inside and had to force herself to concentrate on what he was saying.

"…so I had cash on hand. Ben Miller owed me a few bucks, too, so I'm not broke. There's more money in a savings account, not that I can get to it."

"Ben sounds likes a good friend," she said, straightening her shoulders.

"Army friends tend to last, especially if you see combat together," he said.

As he pulled back onto the highway, Annie handed him a cup of black coffee and stirred a sugar packet into hers. They concentrated on the donuts for a while and then Annie said, "What's the plan for when we reach Reno?"

"I'll take you home. Then I'll go get Megan and leave town again. In and out before anyone knows I'm even there."

"If you're right and Curly and Moe know your ex and your daughter live with your ex-mother-in-law, they'll be staking it out, right?"

"Curly and Moe. The thugs?"

"Yep."

"Okay, you're right, they could be staking out the place."

"But they don't know me."

This earned her a quick turn of the head. "What did you say?"

"They know my name, but I've never met them or Shelby Parker or anyone else connected with this situation. They don't know what I look like. I could show up and make sure Megan is okay."

He narrowed his eyes and said nothing.

"Think about it," she said, stuffing the empty coffee cups into the paper sack that had once held the donuts.

"I don't have to think about it," he grumbled as they crested a hill and started down the other side toward the outskirts of Reno. "It's a lousy idea. You don't know they don't know what you look like."

"And you don't know that they do." She was quiet for a second as the truck rambled along going two-thirds the speed of every other vehicle on the road.

"Where are you going to stay in Reno?" she asked.

"I'll get a hotel down near the tracks. The cops

expect down-and-outers to stay there. I'll keep growing this beard and—"

"Stay with me."

This earned her another long look. He finally said, "Annie, I'm beginning to think you have very poor survival instincts."

"I thought the same thing myself just yesterday. Plus, you might as well know up front that I'm a terrible judge of men."

"What does that mean?"

"It means I pick losers."

"What kind of losers?"

"All kinds. The last one was a gambler. The one before that had forgotten to actually get a divorce. There was the guy who couldn't keep a job, the beer guzzler—"

"I get the picture."

"This time I've circumvented the whole thing. This time I haven't picked a man, I've picked a child."

Another look while a tour bus whipped around them. He said, "Are you actually calling me a child?"

"No," she said, laughing. "I'm trying to say I want to help your little girl. I want her to have her daddy. I think I was wrong to try to atone for my mistake with my father by helping his wife, I think what I need to do is help your child."

"So, now you're comparing me to your father," he said dryly.

She swallowed a big clump of tears she hadn't realized had gathered in her throat. Struggling to keep her voice even, she said, "My father found out about your ex by whatever devious method he used, then he staked out her house like I did the grocery store yesterday in Poplar Gulch. Right?"

"Most likely. Maybe he knew it was Megan's third birthday."

"Yeah. So he figures if you're going to show up, that would be the day. And sure enough, you do."

"But I spent hours waiting for Megan to come out of the house," Garrett said.

"And then you talked to her—"

"No. Absolutely not. I couldn't risk that. Her mother and grandmother were with her anyway, and I knew I couldn't show my face. I just wanted to see her."

"So, my father watched you watch the house until Megan appeared."

"I guess so. I only saw her for a minute before she got in the car and they all drove away."

"In other words, you drove hours to get there and then spent additional hours waiting, just for a glimpse of her."

"I hadn't seen her in months. I was worried sick

Tiffany had decided to cut her losses and put Megan into foster care. I had to know she was okay."

"And while you waited, my father probably used the time making calls to see if he could track down who the truck you were driving was registered to."

"I suppose so."

"And after that, when he couldn't follow you because of the accident and he thought he knew where you lived anyway, he came to see me, he tried to be friendly in his clumsy way. He tried to spend time with me."

"I guess."

"Because of you, Garrett. Because of what he saw you doing, what he saw you risking, all for a mere glimpse of your child. I think he understood what seeing her, even for just a moment, meant to you."

"I don't know—"

"And it shamed him. He'd wasted years. But suddenly, he knew he had to try. And because I rebuked him, I lost his last few hours." She paused for a second and squared her shoulders, charged with resolve. "Well, I can't change the past but I can make it up to him. I can help you. I took a week off work so—"

"Annie, for God's sake, I'm a wanted man. You're breaking the law now, but if you—"

"Don't try to take this away from me," she warned him. "Besides, you need help."

"You've got it all figured out."

"Well, no," she said.

"You understand you could get caught in the crossfire, just as you did up at Ben Miller's cabin, don't you?"

"Yes," she said as their eyes met.

"These people play for keeps."

"I know they do, Garrett," she said, the smell of smoke suddenly filling her nostrils.

They both looked away.

Chapter Six

It went against every grain in Garrett's body to put Annie at risk. The big heart that had her searching for a way to make it up to her dead father was the very same heart that had decided to trust him. And yet he needed help, at least for the rest of that day because she was right, he couldn't go marching into his ex-mother-in-law's house and take Megan. If the house was being watched, Megan might be hurt coming or going or he could be followed—the risks were too great.

Another thing Annie had mentioned finally floated to the surface. She'd said the goons had mentioned wanting "something." He'd quizzed her about it again, but she'd remembered no additional clues as to what this something might be.

He hadn't taken anything that wasn't his. For that matter, he hadn't taken much that was, there hadn't been time. So what had they decided a fire would destroy?

And had it?

More unanswered questions.

Annie lived in a small village outside of Reno, not more then five miles from Tiffany's mother's place. The village was old, one of those small towns that are eclipsed by nearby population centers, peopled with students and seniors looking for cheaper rents.

Her cottage was in with seven or eight other cottages tucked in behind a new apartment building. He dropped her off by her gray hybrid car, which was parked under an awning, and watched as she made her way back to one of the cottages, which she unlocked. She'd told him where he could park the hay truck with the telling California license plates, a block or two away at a yard that stored vehicles for a monthly fee.

Within a half hour, he'd walked back to her place, pretty sure he hadn't been followed or spotted. His leg had hurt a lot at first, the pain kind of receding as he moved, giving him the first hope in months that it was actually going to stop hurting altogether one of these days.

She'd left the door open—the woman was way too trusting.

"Annie?" he called.

"Just a second," she responded from behind a closed door.

Her cottage looked like her, sunny and full of life. She favored primary colors which made him think of a schoolroom, which seemed appropriate seeing as she was a preschool teacher. A decorated Christmas tree in front of the window dominated the living space. There were piles of presents under the tree and he wondered who they were all for or from. Two kitchen shelves were crowded with what appeared to be a cookie jar collection.

The flowery soap fragrance permeating the air was explained a moment later when Annie emerged from the bedroom with damp hair combed behind her ears. She'd used another slew of little clips, purple ones this time, that went with her T-shirt and black slacks, clothes that hugged her curves. She looked young and impossibly fresh.

His gaze zeroed in on her peachy lips. He realized he'd left it there too long when he finally met her eyes and she glanced away, cheeks flushed. "I couldn't go over there smelling like smoke," she said, walking quickly to the kitchen, stepping around him as though afraid to get too close. Was she having second thoughts about him? He wouldn't blame her if she was.

"Listen, Annie, sometimes what seems like the best idea in the world has a way of losing steam when you think about it a little more," he said, filling up the archway separating the kitchen from the living room, leaning against the wall.

She opened the refrigerator and said, "Eggs okay?"

"Eggs are fine. I appreciate the meal. Afterwards, I'll be on my way."

"While I make them, why don't you go wash up? I can't offer you anything clean to wear. Nothing here would fit you."

"That's okay. I'll—"

"Then we need to put our heads together and come up with some sort of plan."

"Annie, now listen—"

Taking the eggs and butter from the fridge, she closed the door with a nudge from her hip and turned to stare at him, eyebrows raised. She said, "Do you have any ideas?"

She hadn't changed her mind, and suddenly he was glad of it. He'd been going it alone for a long time.

"I might have one or two," he said. "I'll go wash up first." He took a few steps and turned back to her. "Do you have any soap that doesn't smell like pansies?"

"For your information, what you smell are gardenias, not pansies," she said, lips curving. "And, no, I'm afraid I don't."

SHE MADE THEM OMELETS with chilies and onions, slathered with superhot salsa and a dollop of cold sour cream. The food came as a surprise as he'd already decided she was the kind of woman who ate club sandwiches. Apparently, he'd been wrong.

He ate in silence, his mind revolving around Megan. The thugs had said they'd stake out the house. That meant he couldn't just waltz up to the door. A phone call would accomplish nothing as Tiffany's mother wouldn't cut him any slack and Tiffany was no doubt still asleep due to working half the night. Not that she'd be likely to help him out, anyway. Wait, she probably wasn't even at her mother's house. No doubt she'd spent the night with her new fiancé, Gary.

They'd have to drive over there and look for themselves without being seen by the jerks who burned down Ben's cabin. He muttered, "That little car isn't going to be any help," and was surprised he'd said it out loud.

"My little car? It gets great mileage," Annie offered, "and it has fewer emissions. Better for the environment."

He stood up and gathered the plates, dumping them in the sink a little too roughly, glad when nothing broke. "There's no way to hide me inside that little thing," he said, turning to face her. "I need something like a van. I can't rent one without showing identification, but maybe you could—"

"Danny next door has an old van. I think it's still got a few miles in it."

"There's an endorsement for you," he said. Narrowing his eyes, he added, "You do know you'll be involving your friend Danny in aiding a wanted man, right?"

"Oh, don't worry, you won't be the first wanted man to ride in Danny's van. Besides, I won't tell Danny anything about you."

He couldn't help the smile that curved his lips. "Using Danny's van, I'll park down the block from Megan."

"We need to get inside the house. I could present myself as some official concerning preschool children. I know it sounds kind of odd, but I have the feeling your ex-mother-in-law isn't the kind who asks a lot of questions."

"You're right about Ellen Boothe. If she thinks she can get some help with Megan, I have the feeling she'll jump on it." It bothered him that he couldn't see Megan himself, that he'd have to rely on Annie for information about her. He couldn't think of a better way, though.

"We'll both need disguises," she said.

Annie went next door to borrow the van, returning within seconds with a key dangling from an empty beer can. Garrett separated the two as Annie dragged him into her room, where he made a big point of not looking at her cozy little bed.

She'd bought herself two wigs, she explained. One was still in the barn, no, correction, had burned up with the barn. She produced a black one still in the box and tried to get him to put it on, but he was adamant. She couldn't go into this situation without a disguise of her own, and black hair was a good start. In the end she humored him. It was amazing what a new hair color did to alter her looks. Leaving the bandage over the bigger wound on her chin, she took off the others and applied makeup. Her eyes got smoky and mysterious, her cheekbones more pronounced, her lips full and plumy.

All in all, he liked her better without the war paint.

Annie disappeared into her closet, emerging a moment later with a hooded gray sweatshirt jacket which she pressed on him. He tugged it on and they both laughed as it was six inches too short in the arms and torso and snug as a second skin. On the other hand, it changed his appearance, which was the whole point.

Her transformation continued with a slinky purple sweater. The color illuminated her face and the fit did wonders for the rest of her, tight across the bust and flared over the hips. The sudden memory of kissing her the night before flooded him with warmth. The memory of her in his arms, her body pressed tight against his chest…

"At least it's cold enough to wear all these layers," she said as she added a trim black jacket.

"Seems kind of hot to me," he said, warm in all the right—or considering the circumstances, wrong—places.

"Do I look official?" she asked, facing him, her expression growing shy, which probably meant she knew exactly where his thoughts had drifted.

"You look perfect," he said. "But I don't like the idea of you driving your own car."

She narrowed her brow in thought for a moment, then brightened. "Mrs. Dodge next door has an old sedan. If I bake her cookies, she'll let me use it."

"Sounds good to me."

As PLANS WENT, theirs was simple. Garrett told Annie where Tiffany's mother lived, then he left in the van. She'd given him her sunglasses to wear and as he left with the hood pulled over his head, she couldn't help thinking he looked like the Unabomber. The plan was for her to follow in fifteen minutes, driving Mrs. Dodge's late husband's blue sedan.

She arrived before eleven o'clock and parked in

front of a small house set back from the sidewalk. She'd passed Danny's van a few houses down the street and had made herself not look to see if Garrett was still in the front seat or not. She saw no signs of the thugs, but then she hadn't expected to. Her theory was simple: any thug worth his salt would be darn near invisible to a novice like her.

Picking a clipboard off the front seat, she slipped out of the car and walked to the front door without looking around or showing her nerves, trying her best to appear like she had an appointment at this house.

The door was answered after a few moments by a woman in her fifties who seemed a little short of breath. The television was on in the background.

"Mrs. Boothe? I'm from the Nevada Preschool Association. You've heard of us, of course?"

Elle Boothe looked as though she'd put in some hard years. Her skin had a faintly yellow cast to it, the whites of her eyes weren't really white. At one time, she'd fought off gray hair with a bottle of dye, but had since given up. Four inches of brownish-gray roots now fizzled into bleached waves. She was a fleshy woman who looked like she wanted a cigarette, a drink and a chair, in that order.

"Never heard of you," she said as she began to close the door.

Annie stuck her foot in the way and said,

"We're offering free, all-day nursery school to children who meet our entrance requirements."

"Free school?" The door stopped closing and even squeaked open a little.

"For children who qualify."

"Her mother ain't here."

"That's okay. I'm authorized to administer a test to Megan Skye. That's her name, right?"

"Yeah, technically, only we call her Megan Boothe 'cause her father's a murdering SOB."

"Fine. May I come in?"

"Sure. Do the kid good to get out with other kids. Lord knows I got enough to do without worrying about a three-year-old."

"I'm sure you do," Annie said.

The house was dark and stuffy, the air heavily laced with stale cigarette smoke. Hadn't the woman ever heard of secondhand smoke and how bad it was for kids? Annie frowned, wondering how to broach the subject and then admonished herself. *Stick to the plan, Annie, don't go off on a tangent.*

A little girl danced through a doorway, singing and twirling, a halo of corkscrew reddish-blond curls bobbing around her face. She wore a lilac tutu and pink tights, a pair of red rubber galoshes on her feet. She promptly bumped into a table and sent a stack of tabloids cascading to the floor.

At the crash, she stopped suddenly, looked around the room and zeroed in on Annie.

"Look what you did, Meg, calm down," Ellen Boothe snapped, turning off the TV. "Sit beside the nice lady and take a test." She looked at Annie and said, "You want coffee?"

Annie didn't want coffee but if it got the older woman out of the room for a while, it sounded like a good idea. She nodded, unable to take her eyes off Megan, who plopped down on the sofa next to her, slipping her hand into Annie's hand. Annie spent her days around three- to five-year-olds and she'd seen her share of cuties, but there was something special about Megan Skye. She had velvety-brown eyes like her father, with a twinkle that radiated curiosity. Her curly hair looked like an extension of the energy her tiny body couldn't contain.

No wonder Garrett craved the mere sight of this child.

"Hello," Annie said.

"I'm this many," Megan announced, struggling to hold up three fingers without the fourth popping up.

"Very good."

"What's a est?"

"A *test*. It's where you answer questions."

She giggled into her hand. "Like what?"

"Like how old you are."

"I'm three." Again with the fingers.

"Okay. And how about your daddy? What's his name?"

Megan wrapped her small arms around herself as though giving herself a hug. She squealed and closed her eyes and said, "My daddy's name is Daddy. I love my daddy!"

"I bet he loves you, too, honey."

"He went way."

"How about Mommy?"

"Mommy goes to Gary."

"But she lives here with you."

"She goes sees Gary a lot."

Annie put an arm around Megan's tiny shoulders. "So Grandma takes care of you," she said.

Megan giggled into her hands again, and then stretched to whisper close to Annie's ear. "Gamma makes smoke comes out her nose."

Annie grinned. "Wow."

"Like a dragon."

"Cool."

Ellen chose that moment to return to the room, balancing two cups of steaming coffee. Annie got to her feet and helped the older woman.

"How's she doing on that test?" Ellen said as she settled into what appeared to be her favorite chair. A television tray set up next to the chair held a dozen little things like cigarettes, a lighter, the

TV remote and numerous capped bottles of prescription drugs that should have been kept out of Megan's reach.

"Just fine." Annie sat back down next to Megan, who once again scooted close. "Megan, can you count to ten?"

Megan scrunched her nose and said, "Six, five, ten!"

Ellen tossed her granddaughter an irritated frown. "Try it again, Meg. This is a test for free school. You can do better. It's on TV all the time."

"That's okay," Annie said quickly. "All we ask is that our students are eager to learn."

"Then she gets in?"

"There are certain standards for the home, as well," Annie said slowly.

Ellen's heavily plucked eyebrows shot up her forehead as she lit herself a cigarette. "Yeah?"

"Safety requirements."

Ellen opened a small brown bottle and shook two capsules into her palm, swallowing them with a noisy slurp of coffee. "Like what?"

"Like keeping dangerous things out of the reach of a child," Annie said and, balancing her untouched coffee, scooped up the prescription bottles and the lighter and carried everything into the messy kitchen, where she deposited the bottles on the back of a counter and the coffee into a sink of dirty dishes. She returned and said, "Keep those things out of Megan's reach, Mrs. Boothe. I'll send you the paperwork in a few days."

Ellen's face reflected her dilemma. She was obviously annoyed at Annie's high-handed behavior but just as delighted with the thought that her granddaughter might qualify for free outside-the-home care. She settled for a grumbled, "Yeah, okay."

"I have to be getting on to my next appointment," Annie said. "No, don't get up, I can let myself out."

She picked up Megan and carried her to the door, standing in the open doorway for a second, hoping Garrett was watching. Megan hugged her with unabashed affection, her curls tickling Annie's nose.

"You come back?" Megan asked in a small voice, staring at Annie's chin. She touched the bandage and added, "You got big owie?"

"Just a little owie. Of course I'll visit again."

"Promise?"

"Yes."

"What's your name?"

"Anastasia."

Megan giggled into her hands again. "That's a silly name."

"I know."

Megan flung her arms around Annie's neck and hugged her fiercely.

GARRETT COULD ALMOST feel his daughter's arms wrap around his own neck. He watched as Annie put her down. The image of Megan waving goodbye as the door closed on her burned itself into his head.

Annie didn't look around as she walked to the old sedan. She got inside, appeared to make a few marks on her clipboard and backed out of the driveway. A moment later, she drove past the black van parked across the street with the magnetic door plaques claiming it was with the electric company. He wondered if she realized the van held Curly and Moe.

At least he assumed that's who the two men were. One was bald, one was hairy, who else? He'd made the van the moment they showed up a few seconds after Annie. He'd started Danny's van and driven past them, noticing in his mirror that they'd hunkered down with fast-food bags, which he guessed explained their absence up to that point. Garrett had circled the block and come back up the alley, parking behind what appeared to be an abandoned house and limping his way through a tangle of an overgrown yard to face Ellen Boothe's house. He arrived in time to see his little girl hug Annie like there was no tomorrow.

Hustling back to Danny's van, he arrived at Annie's place after she did, but not before watching to see if she was followed. He took a circuitous route to make sure he wasn't followed, either.

She'd left her door open again. "Annie, you've got to lock the door," he called, closing it behind him and switching the dead bolt. She came from the bedroom, black wig gone, reddish hair glistening around her freshly washed face.

"I didn't lock it because I knew you'd be right behind me," she said. She broke into a brilliant smile before adding, "Your Megan is absolutely adorable. She's just wonderful. I can't believe how sweet she is and that hair of hers—"

"You're preaching to the choir," he said. "Can you help me get out of this damn sweatshirt?"

"Sure," she said as he tugged on the zipper. While she pulled on the sleeves, he rolled his shoulders and eventually, between the two of them, the fleece all but peeled away. As she dropped the jacket onto the chair, he caught her arm and she turned to face him.

"How was she?" he said. "I mean, did she seem, happy?"

"She seemed good, Garrett. Happy, affectionate. It'll do her good to get out of there soon, but you know that. Ellen Boothe isn't really into little kids."

"Yeah," he said.

"But yours is resilient, fluttering around in a

tutu and galoshes, singing to herself. She's just adorable. I think I already said that."

He nodded once, looking over her shoulder, swallowing the sudden lump in his throat. Annie touched his chin and he met her gaze. "She squealed and hugged herself when she thought of you," she added.

He smiled slowly, a bittersweet tear-at-the-heart kind of smile. He had a lot to make up to his little girl; he'd done just about everything wrong. How had his best of intentions turned out so terrible?

After he'd been released from the army, he'd found himself once again without structure, and the first thing he'd done was look up a girl he'd dated a couple of times before the service. Tiffany Boothe, living in L.A. with dreams of becoming a model. They'd gone out a few more times and the next thing he knew, they were married. It all just kind of happened.

It wasn't until she got pregnant and went ballistic that the seriousness of it all really sank in. And since Megan's birth and Tiffany's relocation to Reno so she could go back to dancing while her mother watched the baby, he'd been trying to get things under control.

Maybe Tiffany didn't want to be a mother, but he sure as hell wanted to be a father. He'd been in the middle of getting it all worked out when Elaine Greason died in a car bomb and life went to hell.

He had to get Megan back. There was absolutely no other option.

Putting her arms around him, Annie rested her head against his chest, snuggling in close to him, her hair a fragrant cloud beneath his nose. He closed his eyes and held her. Had a woman ever before offered him this kind of simple, uncomplicated comfort? Probably his mother when he was little, before she turned into a lush and he turned into a first-class brat. But since then?

Thing was, he didn't want to use Annie or hurt her. He'd be gone in a day or two at most, and he'd never see her again; it would be best if she forgot he ever lived. He was on the cusp of telling her this when all the little man/woman sensors nature had programmed into him clicked on as though a switch had been flipped.

The firm pressure of her breasts against his chest and the soft roundness of her bottom beneath his hands began to get to him. The smell of her skin, the silkiness of her throat, her sweetness, all the ripe possibilities of her, the discoveries waiting to happen, put an edge on the comfort. The feelings were exciting and a little scary, a new mix for him.

He buried his face against her neck and kissed her ear, his fingers pressing into her cloth-covered rear, bringing her closer, anticipating…

"About last night," she said softly.

"Last night?"

"At the barn."

"Ah."

"When you kissed me—"

Smiling, he ran a finger along her cheek to the corner of her mouth. "You mean when you threw yourself at me?"

"Yeah. Well, I was a little…overstimulated."

"True. You'd just escaped a fire."

She nodded. "Exactly. And you rescued me like some dashing hero out of a movie. It all kind of went to my head."

A smile twitched the corners of his mouth. "Are you trying to tell me you aren't really a wanton hussy?"

She nodded again.

"Damn," he said.

"Don't get me wrong, I can be wanton as all get-out."

"Of course you can. I can tell."

"You can?"

"You're a hell of a kisser." He didn't mention the other parts of her that stimulated him because she actually looked embarrassed.

"I just didn't want you to get the wrong idea."

"Because you came on to me last night and then insisted I stay here tonight?"

She chuckled to herself and shook her head. "Yeah."

"In other words, I'm sleeping on the couch."

She nodded again. He recalled the way she'd admitted she picked losers and lo and behold, here he was. It was a sobering thought.

"Why did you come back to the cabin last night?" she asked.

He pushed her thick hair away from her neck so he could admire the soft contour of her jaw as he said, "You want the truth?"

"Of course."

"I just got worried about you. I felt bad for tying you up, bad for leaving you after you'd gone through a car accident, worried that some lowlife would show up and give you a bad time…"

"And they did," she said.

Her velvety soft lips mesmerized him. They were the kind of lips he loved, full and luscious, meant to be nibbled and licked and bruised. He lowered his head even farther, knowing what they tasted like, anxious to experience them again.

She turned her head a little.

"I'll have to work on your resistance," he whispered against her cheek. "It'll have to be a crash course. Now that I know Megan is being watched, I need to figure out how to get her away from Reno without anyone getting hurt, including you."

She drew back a few inches and said, "Why would I get hurt?"

"Sooner or later, someone will associate you with me. I can't put you in any danger. I won't put you in danger."

"That sounds good to me," she said with another smile. "But I don't agree with you."

Puzzled, he wrinkled his brow and said, "What? What don't you agree with?"

"You taking Megan." As he started to protest, she held up a hand and took a few steps. "Hear me out," she said, sitting on a corner of one of the chairs.

And because he'd allowed her life to become so closely intertwined with his, he gave her the benefit of a doubt even though his feet itched to carry him out the door. He sat on her red sofa and said, "Shoot."

"Garrett, it's just what you're proposing is no life for a child, especially not one as full of light as your Megan. Hiding all the time, never seeing her mother or grandmother again. It's not good."

"If you knew Tiffany the way I do—"

"I understand she's not going to win any parenting awards."

"She doesn't want Megan. She as good as tried to sell her to me to get a little nest egg so she could marry some clown named Gary. That's why

I was working for Greason, to earn the dough to buy off Tiffany."

Annie looked startled. After a second, she said, "Be that as it may, think what you're proposing: taking Megan away in the dead of the night, taking her away from everything she knows."

"And what would you say is the alternative to that?" Some of the irritation and frustration he felt with his life bubbled to the surface.

She took a deep breath and then spat it all out in one breath. "You have to prove you're innocent and then take custody of Megan and give her a real home, preferably in a smoke-free environment."

Standing abruptly, he said, "Prove I'm innocent? How do I do that?"

"I don't know," she said. "But that's what you have to do."

He was about to snarl something, but stopped himself. Was she right? Would he hurt Megan if he took her away?

"You were a soldier once," Annie said. "You saw combat. If you could fight for a concept, why can't you fight for the most important person in your world?"

"I am fighting for her," he said.

"I know. I know you are. I'm just asking that you consider what's best for her in the long run."

The long run. Not his strong suit. He was more

the kind of guy that solved a problem now. He'd been laying low for months, getting his leg well. His gut said take Megan and disappear into the woodwork. His gut didn't care about the following years spent looking over his shoulder, condemning Megan to false identities.

That was territory for his brain. Maybe it was time to use his brain and not rely on his gut. The stakes were huge.

He stared into Annie's unflinching eyes and he realized that somewhere deep inside himself was another reason to stand and fight and that was to justify this woman's faith in him. He'd never known anyone besides his brother Brady who looked out for people the way it appeared Annie did.

"Let me think on it," he said.

She nodded once. "Okay."

"The first thing I need to do is get Curly and Moe away from Megan's house." He would think this all out, but first things first. "If you call Shelby Parker and tell her I mentioned going off somewhere, say to Colorado or Oregon, she might give up having the house watched."

Annie stood up and took off the black jacket, revealing the slinky purple sweater beneath. She caught the unconscious direction of his gaze and laughed.

"I'm just looking," he said. "You can't blame

a guy for staring. You're a hell of a good-looking woman."

"I am?"

"Don't you have a mirror?"

"I'm the girl-next-door type," she said.

"Nothing wrong with that."

Smiling, she said, "I'll call Shelby right now."

"Maybe we should iron out the details first."

She retrieved the cell phone from the charger and sat down at the table. "I do things like this better if I don't prepare too much."

He pulled a chair up next to hers. She punched in the number. Their eyes met as the phone rang on the other end.

"Hello?" He could hear the woman's voice clearly as Annie had turned the volume up before placing the call.

"Ms. Parker?" Annie said.

"This is she."

"This is Jack Ryder's daughter."

"Oh, yes. I was going to call you."

"My father—"

"Let's cut the bull," Shelby Parker said. "I know your father is dead."

"How did—"

"Furthermore, he's been dead for several days. Was my mother's killer ever in Poplar Gulch or were you just trying to scam more money?"

"Of course he was there." Annie paused for a second, and Garrett got up to snag a piece of paper and pencil off her counter. He didn't want her admitting any knowledge of the two henchmen or throwing out accusations of her own. The less Shelby Parker suspected Annie knew, the better. He started to write, but she went on without him.

"Skye and I crashed into each other at the top of his driveway, totaling both cars. By the time I regained conscioiusness, he was long gone. A friend came and picked me up. I think Skye might be headed to Oregon. He's from up there somewhere."

Man, she did think fast on her feet. He was seriously impressed. She added, "I can follow—"

"Not on my money," Shelby Parker snarled. "I want a full refund. The contract specified your father deliver the goods and he obviously didn't."

Annie looked at Garrett, who shrugged.

"We'll need to discuss this."

"Fine. Drive east of Sparks about thirty miles. There's a retreat called Hidden Hill. You know the one I'm talking about?"

"Yes."

"Good. I'll expect you—"

"No," Annie said. "I'm sorry, but I'm not going to drive that far, I don't have the time. Meet me in downtown Reno."

There was a slight pause during which Annie

and Garrett stared intently at each other. He wasn't sure why she'd refused to meet Parker in some remote location, he was just glad she had.

"Where?"

Garrett scribbled a name Annie read. "The Golden Hind Casino."

"In a couple of hours?"

"Yes, say 2:00 p.m." Garrett wrote some more which she read before adding, "There's a bar next to the sky bridge."

"As you wish. Though why I should—"

"I'll see you then," Annie said and clicked off the phone.

"That woman is scary," Annie said.

"She sounds like her mother, all confidence and attitude." He studied Annie for a moment before adding, "If Shelby Parker lives in Arizona, how is she going to meet you in downtown Reno in less than two hours?"

"I have no idea. Maybe she's staying at the retreat she mentioned."

"Why isn't she in Arizona going to school? It's too early for Christmas break."

"Why don't I ask her in two hours?"

Garrett smiled but he had another question.

Parker hadn't asked Annie how she would identify her. Did that mean she already knew what Annie looked like?

Chapter Seven

An hour later he was in the Golden Hind wearing a new disguise. Dressed in slacks and a surprisingly good quality sports jacket he'd picked up at a secondhand store, he also wore a scarf around his neck and thick glasses. His beard was beginning to itch. He hoped he looked like some out-of-town businessman who'd spent the last twenty-four hours drinking and gambling and was now nursing the hair of the dog at the bar. He sat in front of a video poker terminal into which he plugged a slow stream of quarters.

No one seemed to look twice at him.

Over the year or so he'd lived in Reno, he'd visited the Golden Hind a few times. The place was named after Sir Francis Drake's famous galleon in which he'd circumnavigated the world in the 1500s. Hence the decor featured a lot of nautical references.

The Crow's Nest Lounge resided next to the sky

bridge on the second floor. He'd vaguely remembered a huge gold mirror behind the bar and had directed Annie to steer Shelby Parker to a table across from it. With any luck, he'd be able to keep an eye on her meeting without being noticed.

Annie showed up on time wearing a snug red skirt, heels and a black sweater, her coat draped over her arm, her lustrous auburn hair pulled away from her face. It was the first time he'd seen her legs. They were shapely enough that several male heads turned to follow her path across the half-empty room.

She didn't give him a second glance and he wasn't sure if she was just assuming they were being watched by a third party or if she didn't recognize him. She hadn't been with him when he bought the new clothes and glasses.

She sat down at a table a little to his right. Within a few moments a waitress dressed in gold lamé took her order and soon returned with a bottle of mineral water.

Not more than five minutes after that, a tall woman with jet-black hair cut blunt around her slender face walked up to Annie and introduced herself. Annie gestured at the seat across the table and the woman he assumed was Elaine Greason's daughter sat down.

Only it couldn't be Elaine Greason's daughter.

Elaine had been Greason's second wife, more than ten years younger than him, a beauty with honey-blond hair and clear gray eyes, forty years old when she died. She'd gotten a little tipsy once and confided in Garrett that she'd had a daughter when she was sixteen. That meant Shelby should be about twenty-two or twenty-three now.

The woman talking to Annie was easily ten years older than that.

The fake Parker waved the waitress away, then leaned toward Annie. She began talking with intense concentration. As Annie responded, the fake Parker brushed her hair behind her ears and looked around the bar, for the first time present-ing a face-on reflection in the mirror. Garrett looked down at the video poker machine at once. He'd seen her somewhere before. Where?

Was it possible he was wrong about Shelby Parker? Had Elaine had a stepdaughter from another marriage? He thought back to all their conversations and couldn't come up with any other daughters. But he'd seen the woman in the mirror before, here in Reno.

Or maybe not in Reno. Maybe not in the flesh. Maybe that's why he didn't recognize her until he saw her entire face.

The meeting broke up a moment or two later. Annie sat back in her chair and finished her beverage. She gathered up her coat and left after that. He waited for a while to see if anyone followed her. If they did, they were better at doing it than he was at detecting it.

He left soon after, letting himself back into her cottage a few minutes later. She raised her eyebrows when she saw his snazzy duds.

"Do you have a computer?" he asked.

"Sure, a laptop. I'll get it."

"So, how did it go?"

"Just a second."

Annie emerged from the bedroom a few moments later wearing jeans and a sweater. She put the laptop on the table.

He sat down in front of it and as she fussed around the kitchen making them something hot to drink, he fired off questions about her meeting while searching the Internet.

"Shelby was older than I thought she'd be. I mean, you told me she was a student. I was expecting someone more my own age but that's stupid because lots of people go to grad school long after they graduate from college." She babbled on happily while filling a teapot from a bottle of filtered water she kept on the small drain board. "I asked her about being in Nevada instead of Arizona and she said since her mother's death she hasn't been able to concentrate so she's taken a leave." Annie set the teapot on a burner and turned on the gas.

"How did she know your father died?"

"She said his obituary was in the newspaper a couple of days ago." She opened the small freezer, peered inside, then slammed the door. "Damn, I'm out of cookies. I need to bake."

"How did your father's obituary get in the paper?"

"Vivian must have forgotten she was supposed to keep it quiet," Annie said. "I'd better call her."

He concentrated on the screen for a few moments before saying, "What did Parker say when you admitted you didn't have her money?"

"She was furious," Annie said. She began searching through a cupboard as she added, "I told her she'd have to get in line if she wanted to threaten my stepmother, so she agreed to wait to see if I could think of an alternative."

"That was nice of her."

"Yeah, well, that's a whole other issue, isn't it? I don't know what to do about Vivian. Mox is going to come asking for his money."

He half heard her as he searched the newspaper's files on Elaine's death. He saw something that triggered a memory and clicked his way to Rocko Klugg's trial coverage.

"I told her I thought you headed north or maybe east," Annie said, her voice coming back into focus. "I told her she should authorize me to finish the job because—"

"Annie, come here," he said, turning the computer toward her.

Carrying a box of tea bags, she leaned close to look at the article on Klugg's sentencing. Her hair smelled like heaven as it fell forward and brushed his cheek.

Klugg was a burly man with very thick dark hair and black-framed glasses much like the ones Annie had worn as disguise. In the photo, Klugg stood in front of a half-dozen microphones. Elaine Greason stood on his right, caught glancing away from the camera.

"Look at the woman on his left," he said. "Does she look familiar to you?"

"That one? Her? Oh, my gosh, that's Shelby Parker, isn't it?"

He looked up at Annie. "According to the caption, that's Klugg's girlfriend, Jasmine Carrabas."

"Uh-oh."

"Klugg's behind it all, I knew it. This is proof."

ANNIE FINISHED the dinner dishes before retreating to the living room. She'd turned on the Christmas tree lights earlier and now sat in her favorite chair admiring the graceful branches and dangling ornaments, most of them given to her by her mother before the airline company she worked for moved her across the country to Boston.

Garrett had left several hours before, taking Danny's van, determined to stake out Ellen Boothe's house until he was sure the thugs had been called off. He seemed very adept at skulking around in the dark. She hoped it came from his years in the army and not from some clandestine post-military activities.

Did she trust him?

Yes. And no. She trusted his heart was in the right place and that he wouldn't hurt her but she didn't trust if the opportunity arose to grab Megan and take off he wouldn't do it. She had the feeling that's how he'd operated for most of his life. She had the feeling he was going along with her now without really agreeing, that he still didn't believe clearing his name was possible and even more than that, necessary if he was going to give Megan a home.

So, he might come back tonight and he might not. She'd make up the sofa just in case.

As for Shelby Parker really being Jasmine Carrabas? After Garrett left, she'd called information and gotten a phone number for Shelby in Tempe, Arizona. With a vague idea of pretending to be conducting some kind of survey, she called the number.

"Shelby Parker," was the prompt reply. Any similarity to Jasmine Carrabas's voice was nonexistent. Shelby sounded like the kind of woman Annie would have as a friend. The pretend survey went up in smoke as Annie couldn't bring herself to lie.

After introducing herself, she said, "Forgive me for bringing up what must be a painful subject, but my father was hired to track down your mother's killer by a woman claiming to be you. I guess I just wanted to make sure she wasn't actually representing you."

"Are you kidding?" Shelby said, her voice going from friendly to guarded. "Someone claimed to be me?"

"My dad was a private investigator."

"I don't know what you're talking about," Shelby said.

"I didn't think you would."

"I can't even imagine…" Shelby's voice trailed off until she added, "Oh. Maybe Robert did it."

"Your mother's husband?"

"Yeah. He was devoted to Mom. Maybe he decided he had to get to the bottom of things, although why he'd use my name… It was the bodyguard he hired who blew up my mother's car, you know. Robert feels terrible about bringing a man like that into my mother's life."

"I didn't know," Annie said slowly, trying to

merge Shelby's image of Garrett with hers. No match.

"Maybe Robert decided to take things into his own hands," Shelby added.

"Maybe," Annie said.

"And maybe I'm to blame."

"What do you mean?"

"I was just up there a couple of weeks ago, clearing some things from my mom's estate, you know like her old safety deposit box and clothes and stuff. Robert and I took a few trips down memory lane. Maybe it reopened some not-very-old wounds. He came down to see me a week or so again and we talked some more. The poor guy is still broken up about it all."

Shelby obviously didn't realize the depth of depravity she was suggesting her stepfather might be guilty of because she didn't know about the recent violence, and Annie wasn't going to tell her. The call had accomplished nothing but to make Shelby feel guilty.

Why hadn't Annie's father figured out Jasmine Carrabas wasn't who she claimed to be when he took the case? Or didn't he care who really hired him? Was he the kind of man content to work for a criminal if it paid enough? Though she didn't know for sure, Annie had to admit it was a distinct possibility. Her father had struck her as a man who didn't trouble himself with a lot of bothersome ethics.

She looked around her cozy little cottage. At the beautiful Christmas tree and the mounds of gifts ready to give to her coworkers and friends. At the window curtains she'd found on sale and the prints she'd framed herself. Home. And yet it was now missing something that it had never missed before and that was Garrett Skye.

In two lousy days he'd stormed into her life—okay, she'd stormed into his—and now there was a six-foot-two-inch, broad-shouldered empty space right in the center of her tidy little world and all at once, everything that had gone on before seemed ancient history.

And yet there was no sign he'd ever been here, he'd taken all his extra clothes with him; the past two days could be nothing more than a wild dream except for the cuts on her face and a lingering ache in her shoulders.

And the hole in her heart.

Garrett might be halfway to Montana by now.

She had to get out of the cottage. Grabbing her car keys and coat, she settled on a shopping trip to replace the eggs she'd used in the omelets. She'd go shopping and then she'd bake cookies for Mrs. Dodge as a thank-you for borrowing the car.

The air outside was crisp, and she hurried off with

a profound feeling of release. This close to Christmas, the store was crammed with people, but they were ordinary people who smiled at her. She hummed along with the relentless holiday music and didn't even lose her temper when someone cut her off at the four-way stop on the way home.

Live and let live. Ho, ho, ho.

When she saw a dark shape pass behind the drapes in her cottage, a smile broke over her face. She'd almost convinced herself Garrett wasn't going to come back and yet here he was. Fleeting visions of baking cookies together, maybe having a glass of wine, filling the house with music and laughter, flashed through her brain followed by the acknowledgment that they had serious matters to discuss.

Anxious to hear if he'd found the goons parked in front of Ellen Boothe's house or caught another glimpse of his daughter, she juggled the grocery bag and dug for her house key as she resumed walking, her step lighter now than it had been before.

There was no need to use the key as Garrett had left the door open for her. She pushed it in quickly, ready to give him a bad time as he'd chided her twice that day for not locking the door. The words died on her lips as her horrified gaze took in what had become of her home.

It appeared as though a tornado had torn right

through the heart of the place, scattering papers, upending furniture, tipping over the tree, gutting her carefully wrapped presents and strewing their contents. Nothing remained of her cookie jars but shards of ceramic and glass.

She'd been gone for less than an hour, she'd locked the door on her way out, she owned nothing of true value. This couldn't have happened in such a short time, her mind couldn't wrap itself around such a pointless invasion....

A noise echoed in the still cottage, the sound of a footstep... how had she forgotten the shadowy shape behind the drape?

The realization came an instant before a figure stepped through the bedroom door. A man wearing black clothing and a ski mask. When he caught sight of her, he lowered his head and charged. Heart leaping into her throat, Annie stumbled backwards, dropping her groceries, ready to scream her lungs out.

Someone grabbed her from behind. She heard a distant yell as her foot hit something slippery and she went down hard, cracking her head on the step, screams dying in her throat.

Chapter Eight

Garrett's leg throbbed. He'd hit it on the gearshift knob more than once as he'd tried to get comfortable in Danny's van. Trouble was the seat in the old clunker was tired, the springs busted, and sitting on it for any length of time resulted in an aching back and the irresistible urge to squirm.

He limped up the path to Annie's cottage with a certain amount of dread. He wasn't sure it was very smart to be back at her place. He foresaw an awkward evening full of long pauses where they pretended not to notice each other, or endless discussions about what to do to clear his name. Both topics depressed the hell out of him.

He'd come damn close to sacking out in Danny's van, but all he needed was a neighbor of Ellen Boothe's growing anxious and calling the cops. A friendly, "Move it along, fella," would turn into a whole other ball game when a cop flashed a light in his face or looked at his ID.

The safest thing to do was come back to Annie's house. So why did it feel so perilous?

The place looked buttoned up for the night, shrouded though the glow of lights behind the drapes was welcoming. His uneven step faltered when he got closer. There was a ripped grocery sack on the ground, spilling groceries onto the sidewalk. Smashed eggs slimed the steps.

He immediately pushed on the door, stopping dead in his tracks. His peripheral vision took in the chaos of the cottage but his focus went directly to the man leaning over Annie's prone body.

In the two seconds it took him to cross the room, the man looked up. Two blue eyes in a pale, bearded face registered alarm. Garrett grabbed the guy by the lapels of his denim jacket, slugged him with a closed fist, and sent him sailing to the carpet next to Annie.

"Dude," the guy called, rubbing his cheekbone as he sat. "Back off, man, I'm the good guy."

Annie looked up at him, her expression dazed.

Garrett knelt beside her, casting the intruder a menacing look that dared him to stand. The guy settled for sitting, knees bent, still rubbing his cheekbone. Heart racing, Garrett cradled Annie's head and looked her over, feeling her head with nervous fingers.

She winced when he came across a tender spot on the back. "Ouch!"

"Annie, are you hurt?" What a dumb question. Of course she was hurt.

She tried to smile and winced.

"Start talking," Garrett said to the other man.

"I just came over to get the keys to my van," he said. He rubbed his eye and added, "Think I'll have a shiner?"

"You're Danny?"

"Yep."

"Wow. I'm sorry. I thought—"

"You thought I was the creep who hit Annie."

Annie struggled to sit. "Don't raise your head," Garrett cautioned. "I'll call for help." Where in all this mess would he find her cell phone to summon an ambulance?

"No," she squeaked.

Danny said, "She wouldn't let me call either."

"Too many questions," Annie said and, wincing again, added, "Could everyone talk a little softer?"

Still holding her in his arms, Garrett said, "Did you see who—"

"No. The one inside wore a mask."

"How about you?" he asked Danny.

"I just saw their backs as they ran away."

Garrett studied Annie's pale face. "You need a doctor."

She managed a weak smile. "In the past two days, I've been thrown from a horse, crashed in a car and jumped from a burning building. If I lived through all that, I can live through this."

"Were you unconscious?"

"I don't think so, not entirely. I was so stupid, I knew someone was in here. At first I thought it must be you, but then I got so caught up in shock at what my house looked like I stood there like an imbecile."

"It's a real mess," Danny said, looking around with a semivacant stare. He gestured at her leg and shoes and added, "You're covered with egg goop."

"Yuck," Annie said.

Garrett said, "Tell me again what happened."

"A man came out of the bedroom wearing a ski mask. Someone else grabbed me from the back. I heard a yell—"

"That was me," Danny said.

"Yeah. I guess it was. I remember slipping and hitting my head and then someone ran over the top of me and I just lay there a while, kind of upside down and scared until Danny showed up."

"It was only a second or two later," Danny said.

"Curly and Moe?" Garrett asked Annie.

"I think so. Who else?"

"Stooges?" Danny said.

Garrett smiled. "More or less. Good thing you came by."

"My turn to make a beer run," Danny said.

It took Garrett a moment to realize Danny

needed his van. "It's out in the lot," Garrett said, handing him the key.

Annie, reaching out to touch Danny, said, "Mrs. Dodge will be afraid to stay alone if she thinks there are muggers on the loose."

Danny stared at her a second, clearly thinking of everything he'd heard them say. In the end, he seemed to give a mental shrug and mimed zipping his lips.

"Thanks for everything," Garrett said, shaking Danny's hand. "If you hadn't come along—"

"Dude," Danny said with a shy glance at Annie.

"Anyway, I put gas in your tank, but all my gear is still in the van. Can I leave it there so it's not in Annie's place?"

"Sure," Danny said. "I'll bring back the key."

"You don't have to—"

"I'm making a beer run," Danny reminded him. "Don't plan on going nowhere tomorrow."

WHILE ANNIE CHANGED out of her dirty clothes, Garrett busied himself sweeping up debris and trying to put right all the crooks had put wrong. It was slow-going work.

This was his fault. Annie was in danger because of him.

"Easy on the poor tree," she said.

She'd come into the room wearing flannel pj's

and slippers. She'd washed her face and still held the ice bag on the back of her head because he'd threatened to take her to the hospital, like it or not, if she didn't.

"Sit down," he said.

She chose the sofa which he and Danny had righted again. He studied her eyes—they seemed okay, no pinpoint irises, no glazed expression—and said, "I think they wanted to make sure you didn't bring whatever it was they burned down Ben Miller's cabin to get rid of back to Reno with you."

"How do you know they weren't looking for you?"

"I doubt seriously they know I'm here. Anyway, if they'd wanted information about me, I don't think they would have knocked you out and left you here without questioning you first. They were just being thorough."

"Danny may have interrupted the questioning period," she said with a shudder in her voice.

That thought had crossed his mind, as well.

She said, "You don't think they'll come back?"

He glanced away from doing his best to rehang the ornaments in time to catch the uneasy shift of her eyes to the front door. "No," he said firmly, though of course he didn't know that for sure. "Look at it this way," he added. "We have to assume Curly and Moe and Jasmine Carrabas are all working together, right? You met with Jasmine, she learned you'd spoken with me. She knew you were in Ben Miller's cabin. Assuming she believes that's true, it's not too big a stretch to picture her sending Curly and Moe over here to make sure you didn't inadvertently or otherwise take from the cabin whatever it is they think I took."

"Which is what?"

"I don't know."

"You didn't take anything from Mr. Klugg?"

"No. I only visited him once and that was in prison."

"How about from Elaine or her husband? Oh, what with everything, I haven't told you I called the real Shelby Parker tonight. I told her there was someone in Reno pretending to be her."

He gave up on fastening the little red ball to the tree. It was one of the few that hadn't broken when the tree fell. "What did she say?"

"She thought it might be her stepfather. Of course, she didn't know about all the violent stuff because I didn't tell her. I have to assume if she did she wouldn't have jumped to the conclusion her stepfather had anything to do with it."

He shook his head. Staring back at the tree, hands hitched on his waist, he thought for a moment before saying, "I didn't take anything from Elaine except for a few castoffs like the pocket watch." He reached in his pocket and pulled out the watch, opened it, turned it around in his hand and wound the stem.

"It was a castoff?"

"Elaine gave it to me when I admired it. She said it had been her brother's and that her husband didn't like pocket watches. She said it had no intrinsic value."

"But maybe she's wrong, maybe it's solid gold—"

"I looked on the Internet and found several just like it for about thirty-five bucks, but even if it was solid gold, the fire was set to destroy something, not recover it."

"True."

He pocketed the watch again, unable to say exactly why it appealed to him so much. Maybe it was the river scene etched on the front, so reminiscent of Riverport, Oregon, his hometown. The bridge looked like one from which he and Brady used to fish. "Anyway, Robert Greason never gave me anything. I don't know what anyone could want."

She pondered what he said for a moment, looking small and injured. God, he felt so guilty he wasn't sure what to do. She wouldn't have been hurt if it wasn't for him.

He had to get out of there, he had to leave Reno. For her sake, he had to cut his losses and run.

The thought was so clear he was sure he'd spoken it aloud, but a glance at Annie revealed closed eyes, relaxed features.

Klugg knew about Annie. He couldn't leave Annie to face these people by herself.

"Where's you father's gun?" he asked suddenly.

Her eyes fluttered open. "In my trunk. I put it there when you let me off this morning."

"I'd better make sure they didn't pop your trunk after they hit you," he said, putting his jacket on and retrieving her keys from where she'd dropped them on the floor. "It's the only weapon we have."

"How about the rifle?"

"That's in the hay truck. I'll retrieve it tomorrow. Right now I'm going to check your trunk."

He got to the door before her voice stopped him. "You are coming back, aren't you?" she said, and once again he heard fear in her voice. He walked back into the room and sat on the sofa beside her. Looking into her eyes, he ran his fingers along her brow, smoothing her hair away from her silky skin. Except for the cut on her chin which she'd rebandaged, the other wounds were now just faint red marks.

When had she become special to him? When

had she gone from cute girl to potential lover to something…else. Something more?

He kissed her forehead. "Of course I'm coming back," he said, and knew from now on, for Annie's sake as well as Megan's, running was no longer an option.

THE CALL CAME as they were eating breakfast. Garrett had made piles of toast and steaming mugs of hot chocolate but Annie didn't have much of an appetite. Facing the bare wall where her grandmother's cookie jars used to sit was too depressing, but the other direction had her facing the living room with its view of the now lopsided Christmas tree missing half its ornaments and the heap of gifts—at least those that hadn't been destroyed—that needed rewrapping.

The caller ID said unknown caller and she didn't recognize the number.

"I'd like to speak to Ms. Ryder," a male voice said.

"I'm Annie," she replied.

"My name is Robert Greason."

Talk about the last person on earth Annie had ever expected to call her! A quick intake of breath was followed by a hasty, "Robert Greason?" mainly for Garrett's benefit. He quietly got out of his chair, walked around the table and sat on his heels next to Annie's chair, wincing as he bent his right leg. She leaned in close so he could hear the conversation.

"You don't know me—"

"I know *of* you," she said.

"I received a peculiar call from my late wife's daughter last night," he said. "She told me you had called her because someone in Reno is impersonating her."

"Someone hired my father to find her mother's killer," Annie said softly.

His voice cracked a little as he said, "Do you know who it was?"

"Not for sure," she hedged. "It's kind of a moot point now, anyway, so—"

"Ms. Ryder, let me be blunt. I want to find Garrett Skye very badly."

"My father is…incapacitated, and I'm not a detective," she said, looking into Garrett's brown eyes.

"I know you're not. I took the liberty of finding out a little about you. I know about your dad. Don't be alarmed. What I was hoping was that you're in some kind of contact with Garrett."

Did everyone know her father was dead? What had Vivian done, taken out an ad? Hoping Garrett forgave her the next comment, she said, "Why would I stay in contact with a killer?"

"Is he? Is he a killer? Are we sure?"

"Your stepdaughter seemed sure. She seemed to think you were sure."

A long pause was followed with a sigh. "I don't know. I just don't know."

"But didn't he shoot someone else right in front of you?"

"Randy, yeah. When Garrett heard the police were coming to talk to him again, he said he wasn't sticking around, he could see the handwriting on the wall, they were going to try to pin Elaine's murder on him. Randy got excited and shot Garrett and Garrett fired back. Oh, I don't know, Ms. Ryder, things aren't quite as black and white as they seemed at first."

"I don't see how I can help you," Annie told him truthfully.

"Please, don't be insulted, I know you're not the kind of woman to consort with criminals. I just want to talk to the man. I want to ask him a few questions. I've been going over things in my mind and then I got a call… If you aren't in contact, though, you can't help me."

"I'm sorry," she said as Garrett caught her free hand and squeezed it. Holding up a finger, he whispered, "Hedge."

"Wait," she said.

"Yes?"

"Uh, let me ask around."

"Would you?"

"I'll try."

"That'd be great. I'll give you my phone number."

"There's no need, it's recorded on the phone."

"Let Skye know I won't turn him over. Tell him I want to ask him questions about what he and Klugg talked about, that's all. I have to get to the bottom of this thing. It's eating me up inside. Elaine was everything to me."

Annie said, "You have to understand it's a long shot. Even if I can figure out where to start, it may take me hours, even days."

"It doesn't matter. It just gives me hope to know there's a possibility. If you're successful, fine. If not, well, thanks in advance for trying."

Annie put the phone down slowly and turned in her seat to face Garrett.

"Did you hear all that?"

"Yeah." He looked thoughtful as he added, "I have to go see him."

"I don't know…this could be a trap."

"Maybe," he said, standing up, "but maybe not. He sounded sincere."

"Maybe he's a good actor."

"Yeah, maybe." He walked back to his own chair, sprawled in the seat and ran his hands through his thick hair. "I have to try."

"For heaven's sake. You're the one always

looking for back doors, take one now. Your instinct to run is a good one. I repeat, this could be a trap."

"How?"

"I don't know. Maybe Jasmine Carrabas told Mr. Greason—"

"Klugg's girlfriend talking to Greason? Unlikely. But even if he did know her, I don't think Carrabas or Curly or Moe have any idea I'm in Reno. And why would any of them think you'd have a link to me?"

"They searched this place last night—"

"And found no trace of me, Annie. I didn't leave anything at your place on purpose."

She had to agree. It was one of the reasons she'd felt he wasn't coming back—he'd left no trace of himself behind.

"If Robert Greason has been mulling this over, I want to know what conclusions he's reached."

"But—"

"And maybe he knows what I have that some-one else wants. Don't you see, Annie, he's the only lead I have."

She leaned forward on her arms and said, "Garrett, please. Think about this."

"I am," he said calmly. "I'm thinking if I want you and Megan safe and I want my life back, the first step is to find out what Greason knows or thinks he knows."

"But—"

"No buts, Annie," he said, leaning forward and grasping her hands. "I have to do this," he said, looking deep into her eyes. "But I'm not an idiot, I'll take precautions. Trust me."

Three hours later, Annie called Greason and told him she'd lucked out, she'd talked to a man in Poplar Gulch who knew how to get a message to Garrett Skye. She'd waited the three hours at Garrett's insistence, not wanting to make it look as though it had been too easy.

If Skye wanted to meet, she told Greason, he'd get in touch with Greason within the day. She'd done all she could.

UNDER THE THEORY the best way to become invisible is to blend in, Garrett put his sports coat back on. By now, the lower half of his face was pretty damn furry and he trimmed it carefully.

Leaving Annie baking cookies behind a locked door—he'd made a run to the grocery store for her—he drove Danny's van past the Boothe house to check for Curly and Moe. The street held few cars and none with anyone sitting in them. Hopefully, the search of Annie's apartment coupled with

Annie's conversation with Jasmine Carrabas had reassured everyone he was a long way from Reno.

From there he drove to a mall where he picked up a prepaid cell phone and a very small tape recorder he slipped into his pocket. He had a heart-jarring moment when a security guard stopped him, but it turned out all the guy wanted to know was the time. His own watch battery had just died.

Garrett had originally considered meeting Greason at the Glistening Sands Casino, where Greason was an executive VP as well as the man who oversaw casino finances. That plan had died a short death, however, as Garrett thought of the logistics of getting in and out the heavily guarded place he'd worked for several months without being recognized. Besides, if Annie was right, the casino would make a dandy trap. Greason's office was on the top floor.

In the end, calling from the parking lot, he asked Greason to meet him at the outlet stores east of Reno. He made the timing such that Greason would have little chance to do more than drive straight there.

Garrett wasted no time losing himself in a sea of holiday shoppers. He was pleased to note his limp had continued to improve to the point it was barely discernable. He visited one or two stores and made purchases so he had bags to carry. A new cookie jar for Annie to replace one of the many that had been broken, a plush reindeer for Megan with bells on the antlers, a hat for himself that he pulled low on his head, thereby joining the other citified cowboys following their women from store to store.

For a second, he paused in front of a poster depicting a family Christmas scene and experienced an unexpected lump in his throat. Father, mother, two kids, a dog, a Christmas tree, tons of presents.

He'd never experienced a Christmas like that and until seeing that stupid poster, hadn't much missed it. Now he was burning with the desire to give Megan what he hadn't had: family.

And that meant his father, if he ever dried out, and Brady and his wife and son, too.

And Annie. It meant Annie.

And yet it didn't because the simple truth was he wasn't good enough for her. *I always pick losers*, she'd said. He didn't want to be her next loser.

A few minutes later, he walked into the deli he'd remembered from a year before, gratified to see it was no more popular now than it had been then, and took a seat at the back where he could watch the door.

Greason arrived on time wearing a long gray coat over his suit. As Garrett pulled the Stetson even lower over his eyes, he thought that Greason wore his fifty-two years well with close-cropped silver hair and lean features, bright-blue eyes and very white teeth, the kind of man they photographed for cognac commercials. He and Elaine had made a striking pair.

Greason paused by the door and looked around the deli, his gaze sliding right past Garrett with only a flicker of recognition. As he walked toward Garrett's table, Garrett flipped on the tape recorder in his pocket before taking off the hat and laying it on an empty chair.

Greason sat down opposite him. Raising one eyebrow, he said, "I almost didn't recognize you. Thanks for agreeing to talk to me."

Garrett wanted to make sure Greason didn't connect him to Annie so he said, "I was on my way through Lake Tahoe when I got your message. By tomorrow, I'll be out of Nevada." He leaned forward a little as he added, "Let's get one thing clear. Whether you chose to believe it or not, I liked Elaine. I had nothing to do with her death."

Greason nodded and said, "I never thought I'd say this, but I'm beginning to believe you."

Garrett kept his surprise hidden as he said, "How is Randy Larson?"

"He's okay. Your bullet went through his thigh without causing any permanent damage. I heard somewhere that he started wrestling again. Calls himself Red Thunder."

Garrett half smiled, relieved he hadn't destroyed the kid's dreams. He said, "Why did you want to talk to me?"

They both looked up as a pale teenager in a dirty apron finally showed up to take an order. They asked for coffee and the girl shuffled off. She was back a few moments later with two cups that splashed onto their saucers when she lowered them to the table.

"I want to know what you and Klugg talked about when you went to visit him in jail a couple of weeks before Elaine died," Greason said, using a paper napkin to dab at the spilled coffee.

"I told him what you asked me to tell him, what Elaine asked. You guys didn't want him contacting her again, she had nothing to say to him."

"What did he say?"

"Not much. Mostly just sat there looking belligerent. Called her a few names." He'd told Greason all this months before.

"And that's all? He didn't mention any papers or…blackmail?"

Blackmail? What was this about blackmail? "What are you getting at?"

Greason pushed aside the damp napkin. "Klugg contacted me last week."

"Okay."

A knot formed in Greason's jaw as it appeared he worked on keeping his temper. "He told me the bomb was supposed to scare Elaine, not kill her."

Garrett furrowed his brow. "What?"

"He said you botched the job."

Garrett dropped his own cup back onto the saucer where it rattled. A surge of hope rushed through his body. "Wait a second. If he said all this then he's admitting responsibility." For the first time in months he saw a tiny spot clear in the clouds above.

"No way," Greason said. "The man is cagey, he never says anything that can't be twisted umpteen different ways. He drove Elaine crazy. He's out of prison now. I see you didn't know. Well, he is. Getting himself a new trial on the original charges because of some legal mumbo jumbo that comes down to Elaine being termed incompetent. It frosts me that a man like that can sully the name of a good attorney. If I could, I'd—"

He paused for a second, the knot in his jaw tightening. Taking a deep breath, he added, "The D.A. is trying to build a case against him for Elaine's death but there are no witnesses. Everyone knows better than to rat on Rocko Klugg." He paused a second before adding, "You know, Garrett, they might cut you a deal if you turn state's evidence against Klugg."

"Except I can't do that because Klugg didn't hire me," Garrett said, irritated with the game Greason seemed to be playing. Trusting him one minute, suggesting he had something to barter the next? He made himself sit there in the diminishing hope Greason had something to tell him that could help.

"You know the cops found an envelope of cash in your apartment?" Greason added. "And that your ex-wife told them you'd been desperate to save enough money to take your kid away from her?"

"Tiffany said that?"

Greason nodded.

Well, what was he surprised about? There was no love lost between himself and Tiffany and of course she'd shade things to make herself look good and him bad. But didn't that mean it was common knowledge that Garrett had a little girl living in Reno? That's how Klugg knew about Megan, that's probably how Annie's father had known about her, too.

As for the stash of money he'd supposedly hidden in his apartment, he'd read about that on the Internet at the Poplar Gulch library. "Since I didn't plant it, I have to assume someone else did. The question is who."

"The same person who called the tip into the cops," Greason said.

"Yeah, well, almost anyone can make a call or pay someone to make a call for them. But who had access to my apartment?"

"I guess Mrs. Simpson. Me. Randy. The gardener. The guy who closed up the pool in September."

"Hard to imagine your elderly cook or any of the rest of them sneaking around," Garrett said.

"Well, I sure as hell didn't do it."

"So, that leaves Randy, but he was in the hospital after I left."

Greason sat back in his chair, his arms folded across his chest. He finally said, "I'm never really going to know what happened to Elaine, am I?"

There was no answer to that. Garrett said, "When did Randy get out of the hospital? Before or after the tip got called into the police?"

"I'm not sure. He went back to his girlfriend's place. You don't think he—"

Garrett wasn't about to blame another man without proof. He shrugged.

Greason cleared his throat and placed both hands palms down on the table as though bracing himself to deliver bad news. Garrett's stomach, already in a knot, tightened. "Listen, you might as well know they also found some electronic gizmo they say is used in making a remote bomb like the one that killed Elaine."

"In my apartment?"

"Not with the money, hidden under the bottom of an old recycling container out back."

"But they didn't find anything the first time they looked. Doesn't any of this sound suspicious?"

"All of it, which is why I'm here," Greason said.

"I still don't understand why Klugg would want to kill Elaine. I know he wasn't happy with her representation, but—"

"I know, I know, it never made sense to me, either," Greason said, "until Klugg told me she wasn't supposed to die. That's where the blackmail comes in." Greason forgot he didn't like the coffee and tried another swallow, this time so preoccupied he apparently didn't notice how bad it was. Lowering his voice, he said, "Klugg claims he gave Elaine an incriminating document she was supposed to destroy, but instead, she used it to blackmail him. Do you know anything about this?"

"No," Garrett said. "Absolutely not. I can't imagine Elaine blackmailing anyone."

"Nor can I," Greason said. "I've looked everywhere but I'm not even sure what I'm looking for. Something with numbers was all he'd say. I can't believe Elaine would keep a secret like this from me and I'm not ashamed to admit I've started looking over my shoulder."

"Go to the cops," Garrett repeated.

"I can't. Klugg threatened to send me to join

Elaine. I believe him. Plus, and I know this might sound crazy to you, but I don't want Elaine's reputation dragged through the mud. She was a respected attorney in Reno, her good name meant everything to her. It's bad enough Klugg won another trial, but if this got out, people would talk..."

"People talking isn't the worst thing in the world," Garrett said with some experience.

"I know. I know." He studied Garrett with anxious eyes as he added, "You were one of the last people to see Elaine alive. You drove her all over hell and back the day before she died."

Garrett nodded. He'd been the last one to drive Elaine's car before it blew up and the only one around who knew anything about explosives. Plus, he was supposed to be behind the wheel that day and he wasn't, he'd called in sick. Mighty suspicious. "We made a lot of stops," he said. "Shopping, her office, the bank."

"Did you guys talk about anything remotely connected to Klugg?"

"She was nervous about him contacting her again and thanked me for going to tell him to back off."

"Did she talk about me? About us?"

There was no denying the emotion in the older man's eyes. Garrett said, "I can't remember what we talked about. Ordinary stuff, that's all."

"That damn Klugg."

Klugg was a piece of work, all right. He'd hired a hit man to take care of two other guys and then claimed the hit man acted on his own. The hit man himself had disappeared from the face of the earth during the trial. That was probably the real reason why Klugg had finagled another go round in the criminal justice system.

"Nowadays, documents can be anything," Greason said, giving up on the coffee again. "And what the hell does 'document' mean anyway? Why isn't he more specific?"

"Probably because just as you said, if it was the content that was important and not the original form, then it could have been photocopied or put on a disk or a microchip or wired…"

"I can't imagine Elaine doing this. If it was incriminating why didn't she turn it over to the cops?"

"Client confidentiality?"

"I suppose. But there's a difference between destroying something and using it to extort—"

"Just because Klugg says she was blackmailing him doesn't mean she was," Garrett said. "The man is hardly reliable."

"Did Elaine give you anything to keep for her?"

"Nothing."

"Did she give you, I don't know, gifts?"

Garrett thought of her brother's pocket watch. There'd also been a pair of onyx cuff links and a couple of books. The books he'd had in his car so they'd traveled with him to Poplar Gulch and were no doubt ashes now. He returned Greason's stare and decided on caution. Curly and Moe had shown up at the cabin looking for something. Jasmine had apparently sent them to Annie's place for the same reason. Now Greason was looking and what all these things had in common was Klugg. At least now Garrett knew "it" was some kind of document.

"There were a few things I left at the apartment at your place," he hedged. He'd left in a hurry, without packing.

"After the cops released the apartment, I had Mrs. Simpson box up your personal things," Greason said. "The box is in my trunk. Frankly, I already looked through it. If it's there, I can't see it."

"I'll take the box, I'll look. But I'll be honest, my main priority is finding out who killed Elaine and proving it. I want my life back."

"Maybe our goals will dovetail," Greason said. "Maybe this document is the real reason Elaine had to die and maybe it will lead to the man who really pushed that button and killed my wife."

"Yeah," Garrett said, his mind already racing ahead to what came next.

"Let me know what you find, if anything," Gleason said. He pushed the half-empty cup away and seemed to shiver as he added, "I don't mean to sound melodramatic, but I truly believe it's a matter of life and death."

So did Garrett.

Chapter Nine

Annie set a plastic plate of mint-chip cookies down on the table and stared at her visitor.

Vivian Beaumont Ryder, dressed in various shades of pink, sipped tea from one of the few cups that hadn't been broken the night before. The anxious twitch of her thin lips revealed she wasn't paying a social call.

That and the two words that slipped out every few moments.

"I'm scared," Vivian said as she picked up a cookie. She'd said it a hundred times since knocking on Annie's door an hour before, but Annie didn't blame her for repeating it. If she owed ten thousand dollars to a loan shark, she'd be scared, too.

Vivian's age was hard to determine. Fifty, sixty? Her hair, and there was a lot of it, was very blond and teased into the stratosphere, perhaps making Vivian feel taller than her five foot one inches.

"I miss your father so," she said, eyes welling with tears. "I didn't even know he had heart problems. One day he's fine, the next he's dead."

Annie thought back to the day her father came to visit and she'd sent him away. Had he looked sick? No.

"I'll tell you this," Vivian said, shaking the cookie at Annie. "If Jack were still here, he'd have caught that murderer and paid off Mr. Mox. Tell me again what you did when you went to California. Besides destroying your father's car, that is."

Annie leaned back against the counter, and said, "I just couldn't find Garrett Skye. I'm a preschool teacher, not a detective."

"But you said you would."

"I said I would try," Annie said gently. "And I did. Was Dad's car insured?"

"That old heap? He only carried liability."

"I don't know what else I can do." Annie paused a second before adding, "You might as well know, Vivian, that the client is demanding a refund of the original advance."

Vivian gasped as her hand flew to cover her heart.

"Don't panic," Annie added hastily, picturing another heart attack. "Dad must have made arrangements to be reimbursed for time and expenses, you know, no matter what the outcome, so it won't be the whole thing. I just thought you should be prepared in case you get a call from her. And you might not. She might decide to chalk it all up to experience. You might want to look for Dad's records, though, just in case."

Who knew what Jasmine Carrabas's next move might be?

Vivian dropped what was left of her cookie into what was left of her tea and fanned her face.

"I think you're going to have to go to the police and ask for protection," Annie said.

"Or leave Reno," Vivian said. She cast Annie a look up through her lashes and added, "You don't happen to have any money, do you, Annie?"

Annie almost laughed. "Ten thousand dollars? No."

"It was your father who got me into this mess," Vivian pointed out.

"That's true."

"Isn't that your car out front? It looks new. Couldn't you sell it?"

The woman might look like spun sugar on the outside, but Annie was beginning to detect a rock-hard passive-aggressive core. Put Jasmine Carrabas, Curly, Moe, Mox and Vivian into a locked room and who knew who would emerge victorious? Annie said, "I don't own the car, my credit union does."

Vivian sighed, looked around the Spartan

cottage and sighed again. Since the break-in had destroyed so many fragile knickknacks, the place looked pretty bare to Annie, too. She swallowed a lump of loss and told herself to keep her priorities straight. She was alive.

"I thought you weren't going to put the announcement of Dad's death in the newspaper," Annie said.

Vivian nibbled on her lip and said, "I didn't."

The oven timer rang and Annie took out the last batch of cookies, calling over her shoulder, "But someone told me they read about it in the obituary section."

"Nonsense," Vivian said. "I don't want Mr. Mox to know Jack isn't among the living. There was no obituary, I made very sure of that."

Annie set the cookie sheet on the drain board. "That's odd."

The sound of a key at the front door sounded loud in the small cottage. She and Vivian both looked up as Garrett entered carrying a sizable cardboard box and a few shopping bags. "It smells great in here," he said, his face hidden behind the box.

He put his load down in front of the sofa and turned to face the kitchen. He wore a black Stetson low on his head. When he glanced at Annie, her heart and stomach seemed to bump against each other.

"I didn't know you had company," he said, smiling at Annie as he took off the hat. She could see the questions burning behind his eyes. He was probably wondering, *now what?*

He had cause to be concerned. If Vivian caught on to Garrett's real identity she might whip out a gun and turn him in herself.

Rushing to meet him, Annie grabbed his hand. "Vivian Beaumont Ryder, let me introduce my good friend Bob. Bob works at the preschool with me."

"Nice to meet you," Garrett said.

Vivian narrowed her eyes. "*You* work at a preschool?"

Garrett slung an arm over Annie's shoulders. "It's the best way to keep an eye on my girl," he said, leaning down to kiss Annie's forehead. "I don't want her running off with some rich four-year-old."

Vivian laughed. She took a deep breath and, straightening her fuchsia blouse, stood up. "I've taken enough of your time. At least my car still runs. I think I'll go visit my mother in Boca Raton."

"That's a good idea," Annie said, handing her stepmother her coat. "She doesn't happen to have any money she could loan you, does she?"

"Not a friggin' dime," Vivian said, "but she's dating a man who's loaded. Maybe he'll help me out." She'd reached the door before she turned. Buttoning her quilted jacket, she looked at Annie with moist eyes and said, "Your father wasn't a bad man. Maybe he worked outside the strict letter of the law on occasion and he shouldn't have gambled so much, but he never hit me and he never took a drink." Her gaze swerved to Garrett then back at Annie before adding, "A woman could do a lot worse than get hooked up with a man like Jack Ryder."

Annie leaned against the door once it was closed and stared at Garrett. "How's that for an epitaph?"

"I guess a man could do worse than have a wife who misses him when he's gone," Garrett said.

His words held the bittersweet note of regret. He had moved to the sofa where he was using his pocketknife to cut the packing tape that held the box closed. She sat on the chair at a right angle to him, clasping her hands between her knees. "Garrett, do you mind my asking you a kind of personal question?"

"No," he said, glancing at her.

"Did you love Tiffany?"

He looked back at the box as he flipped open the first flap. "I thought I did." Another slice, another flap. He laid the knife aside and added a little muscle power as he said, "Maybe I just had the hots for her. I was stupid enough where I might have confused the two."

"But you wouldn't confuse them now?"

He smiled in his slow way, the way that seemed to take a week, the way that melted her. She'd resolved to keep her distance from him, but when he set aside the box and reached out for her, she allowed him to tug her over to the sofa to sit beside him.

"I think I'm beginning to see there are deeper aspects to relationships," he said.

The pressure of his thigh pressed against hers had her on edge. As he stared into her eyes, she found herself having trouble forming a coherent thought. He said, "With Tiffany, I understood lust. I understood wanting someone. But now I see it was the other stuff I didn't know about that was missing with her."

"The other stuff?"

"Like caring about her more than I cared about myself. Like wondering what she'd say next, what she'd do next. Wondering if she was okay, if I could make things better for her. Or if I was only making things worse."

"Caring," she whispered, her fingers resting atop his arm.

"Caring about what comes next," he said, still gazing deep into her eyes.

"Sometimes, lust comes first," she said softly.

"I know." Almost reluctantly, it seemed to Annie, he cupped her chin, ran his thumb slowly over her lips, his fingers stroking her jaw, caressing her throat, lingering, hot and strong, traveling down her neck, over the contours of her breasts. His movements were so firm and purposeful it made the skin under her clothes sizzle with anticipation. By the time his hand smoothed over her belly and came to rest at the point her groin met her thigh, she was ready to jump out of her skin.

He raised her hand to his bearded face and kissed her fingers. When he paused, she continued the same journey along his face he'd made on hers, touching him as though she planned on sculpting his image with her eyes shut, moving her hand across the tantalizing muscles beneath his shirt to his rock-hard abs and flat stomach, barely brushing the denim-covered erection tight against his jeans, hard beneath her hand. A jolt passed through her fingers right into her core as her gaze flew up to meet his.

He stared at her lips for a moment, a moment she spent wishing he'd kiss her, wishing he'd ravish her, wishing he'd pull her into an embrace and give her no option but to abandon reason and thought.

But he took a deep breath instead. "What am I going to do about you?" he said, taking her hands in his and gently folding them together inside the warm cocoon of his grasp. "I'm full of good resolutions until I get near you and then, whoosh, everything goes out the door."

"Is that so bad?" she whispered.

He nodded.

"For you or for me?"

"For both of us," he said slowly. "You told me what kind of men you choose. At the moment, I think you'd be hard-pressed to find a bigger loser than me."

"I don't agree with you," she said.

His upper lip twitched as he said, "I know you don't. And that, sweetheart, just makes you all the more irresistible."

"Well, at least you think I'm irresistible, that's something," she said.

"I think you're wonderful," he said so softly she had to strain to hear. "Beautiful, inside and out. Loving, caring. You deserve a man who can give you the world, not one who can only take from you."

"But, Garrett—"

"Let me have my pride," he said. "Don't argue with me. This is hard enough as it is."

They stared at each other for a second more, then she withdrew her hands from his. If that's the way he wanted it, that's the way it would be. She'd more than nudged the door open, she'd hung out a welcome sign. In her head she knew his caution was justified. In her heart, well, that was another story.

Swallowing a sigh, she said, "Tell me what happened with Mr. Greason," and strove to sound matter-of-fact. She gestured at the box and added, "What's all this?"

"This is the personal stuff I left in Greason's apartment," he said, obviously as anxious as she was to move away from the volatile issue of their mutual attraction. "Hold on a second." He got to his feet as though happy for the excuse to move and retrieved a tape recorder from his jacket pocket. After he rewound the tape, he settled back on the sofa a few inches farther away from Annie than before. Holding the recorder between them, he turned it on.

"I can't make up my mind if he believes you or not," she said when it was over.

"I don't think he can either," Garrett said.

"Klugg claims the bomb wasn't meant to kill her. Do you believe that?"

"Considering how little there was left of the car, I don't know."

"I wonder why Klugg is still naming you? Why not admit who it really was? What does it matter to him?"

"He's invested all this time and trouble into framing me. All he wants now is whatever Elaine took from him."

"And both men seem to think she gave whatever it is to you."

"Because I was the last person to spend any time with her. Does that make sense? I don't know."

"So why, after almost four months, did Klugg hire my father to find you and threaten Mr. Greason? Why not before? If this item has been missing since Elaine's death, why did he just start looking now?"

"Good questions," Garrett said. "I guess he assumed Elaine gave it to me, and so disappeared with me. Maybe he assumed the police would find me but when they didn't, decided to take matters into his own hands—"

"About the time he got out of prison for a new trial?"

"That's right. Now he's making sure whatever he's missing went up in the fire that destroyed Ben's cabin. Covering his bases." He lifted out two books, handing one of them to her. "I don't know what to tell you to look for, just look."

The onyx cuff links turned out to be nothing more devious than sterling silver and onyx, the CD cases held music discs, the labels inside covered with lyrics and production information, as promised. There were no secrets sewn into the hem of his jeans, rolled into his socks or tucked in between the pages of his books. His laptop had no battery power and the charger cord was missing.

"You'll have to replace the cord before you can check your laptop," Annie said.

"Elaine was never even in my apartment. I doubt she knew I had a computer."

"How about e-mail?"

"I let my account go when I left but it doesn't matter because Elaine never sent me anything." He shoveled everything back into the box and added, "It's all a big, fat zero."

"Which leaves the watch," Annie said. He dug it out of his pocket and handed it to her. As she traced the slight corrosion on the back with her thumbnail, she said, "Garrett, you're not worried about Elaine's good name, are you?"

"Hell, no. I'm concerned with Megan's future and your safety. If Elaine was doing something illegal, then it'll come out. If Greason doesn't like it, too bad."

She was relieved to hear that. "You have a tape now with Mr. Greason explaining Klugg's role in his wife's death. Isn't that enough to take to the police?" As she spoke, she attempted to pry loose the back of the watch, which proved impossible.

"Klugg claimed I was his accomplice, remember?" Garrett said.

"What about Randy Larson? Maybe Mr. Greason is wrong, maybe Randy had the opportunity to plant that money. Maybe he still had a key and snuck back."

"Maybe he did more than that," Garrett said.

"What do you mean?"

"Bombing Elaine's car was an inside job. If it

wasn't me then it was one of the others at that house and that includes Randy."

"I can't get this open," Annie said, handing him back the watch.

"I can't either. I haven't had time to take it into a shop to see if someone can get it open without busting it. Elaine said it would be garbage if it ever stopped working because its value would be far exceeded by the cost of repair."

"Does it keep the time well?"

"Perfectly."

"And it's special to you. Because of her?"

He looked up from winding it and furrowed his brow. "Not really. It's the front of the thing, I guess, the etching. The river reminds me of home and my brother. Plus, I guess I like the substantial weight of it, the fact it has to be wound."

"It's old-fashioned," she said.

"Yeah. Like something a father would give a son."

She wondered if he heard the longing in his voice. Was that what was really behind his attachment to the old watch, the fact that it felt like something connected to the past even if it wasn't his past? Her heart went out to the boy who still lived inside the man's heart.

"So, what's next?" she said softly.

"I go talk to Randy."

"But if he's guilty of anything—"

"He'll try to deny it. But Randy is a lousy liar. The kid has one of those open faces."

"I want to come with you."

"He may be simple, but he's big and if he has something to hide, he could be dangerous," Garrett said.

She shrugged as she looked around what had always been her little haven. The afternoon was fading; it would soon be night. "I guess I don't feel real safe alone in this cottage right now," she admitted. "I keep expecting a visit from someone I really don't want to see like Curly or Moe. I'd like, well, I'd rather be with you."

His expression softened as he looked at her. "I'll make a few calls, try to pin down where he is," Garrett said, taking out his new phone.

"But you won't warn him you're coming, will you?"

"Absolutely not."

"I'll put the cookies away." Annie hopped to her feet. She got halfway to the kitchen when she stopped. The bare shelves running along the kitchen walls reminded her she had nothing in which to store them except plastic bags, which were good for Mrs. Dodge's share, but what about the rest of them? At that moment, there was a tap on her shoulder and she turned to find Garrett.

"Merry Christmas, Annie," he said, and handed

her one of the shopping bags he'd brought into the cottage with the box. She opened it to find a pottery cookie jar shaped like a brown horse.

"It kind of looks like Scio, doesn't it?" he said, smiling at her.

She touched the smooth ceramic jar and looked up into Garrett's warm brown eyes. "Oh, Garrett," she said and, to her horror, burst into tears.

"HE'S TRAINING at a gym about twenty miles from here," Garrett said a half hour later after a dozen calls on Annie's phone. "His girlfriend couldn't remember the name of the place, just that it was in back of the Twilight Tavern. I remember it, though, and if I'm not mistaken, it's an RKI gym. The girlfriend said he'd be there until seven."

"What's an RKI gym?" Annie asked as she idled at a red light. The pre-holiday meets rush-hour traffic was brutal.

"Rocko Klugg International. I told you he owned a string of gyms or training centers as he liked to call them."

"So Randy is training at a place owned by Rocko Klugg. That's interesting."

"Isn't it?"

They were quiet for a few blocks, then Annie said, "I hope you don't mind, but before Vivian got to my place, I called Mrs. Boothe."

He stared at her profile a moment before saying, "Why?"

"I asked her a few questions under my Nevada State Preschool persona, just to check that everything was okay. That Megan was okay." She flashed him a uncertain smile and added, "I could hear her singing in the background."

He briefly touched her leg. "Of course I don't mind. I drove by there, myself. No Curly or Moe."

"Tell me about your last day with Elaine," she added as she took the freeway ramp going east. "On the tape it sounded like you did errands all day."

Garrett looked up from stowing his duffel bag under the seat. Inside the bag was Annie's father's gun, just in case. He said, "She was looking for an antique letter opener for her father's birthday. He collects the things. She had a line on a bronze and ivory one down near Lake Tahoe."

"Did she buy it?"

"No. She took a few pictures of it, but I don't think she could make up her mind."

"What else did you do?"

"Let's see. She needed to stop by her office to do a little catch-up Saturday work and then she wanted to shop in a department store so I followed her around for a while."

"Where did she shop?

"Downtown Reno. Casey's."

"Then you went to one of the downtown banks?"

"No, a little branch out east of Sparks."

"That seems like an odd place for a busy woman to do her banking."

"It had originally been her brother's bank. He put her name on his safety deposit box. After his death, she started banking there, too. She got the watch and cuff links and the books out of her safety deposit box and gave them to me. Like I said before, they belonged to her brother."

"Why would she give them to you?"

"Greason isn't the kind of guy to carry around an inexpensive watch or wear old cuff links. Or read fiction, for that matter."

"We're back to the watch," Annie said, casting him a quick look.

"Or the cuff links. Or neither." He gestured toward a sign and said, "Take the next exit."

"She might have put something in the box the day she took something out," Annie said as she made the turn. "Like maybe money from blackmail?"

"Maybe. But wouldn't whoever inherited wonder about a stack of cash?"

"You'd think so. Maybe you should mention you took Elaine there specifically so Robert or Shelby can look at the contents more carefully."

"I told Robert I took her to the bank."

"Did you say which bank?"

"I don't remember. Turn right at the next light."

She was quiet for a few minutes as she fought the heavy commuter traffic. She finally said, "Did anyone ever look into Mr. Greason as a suspect for his wife's murder?"

"Like he hired me or someone else to plant the bomb?"

"Or did it himself."

"I guess they always suspect the spouse. But he had nothing to gain from her death, their finances were separate and he actually seemed more financially secure than she was. On the morning Elaine died, he was in the kitchen drinking coffee in full view of Mrs. Simpson and some guy who'd brought a bunch of papers from the casino for him to sign. In other words, his hands were in plain view, he didn't push a button on a remote."

"Why did they settle on you so quickly?"

"We'd all had a barbecue the night before," Garrett said, remembering that warm August afternoon as about the last normal time he'd experienced. Greason had been expansive, grilling steaks, Elaine had danced with Randy, even Mrs. Simpson had unwound as she sipped wine. Elaine had said it was a celebration though she wouldn't say of what. All that had been missing—as far as Garrett was concerned—had been Megan.

The next morning, Elaine had started her car and it had blown up right there in the driveway, taking out part of the garage, as well. The day after that, Garrett had received word the police were coming back to question him again, he'd decided to run, Randy had shot him, he'd shot back and life had changed forever. His leg sent him a little wake-up tinge.

"Garrett? Did I lose you?"

"Sorry. I didn't feel very good the next day," he said. "Because of that, Elaine ended up in her car alone. A few minutes later, it blew up."

"So it looked as though you avoided being in the car."

"Exactly. And now that Tiffany sold me down the creek and the money and electronic stuff showed up at my place, it looks worse than ever."

"Yes, it does."

He slid her a look. He hated the thought she might start to wonder about his innocence. How could she not?

She said, "Someone wanted to make sure you got all the blame, didn't they?"

"Yeah," he said, grateful beyond words for her support. He hadn't really earned it, she'd just given it to him. Where did a person learn to be that generous?

"This should be about the right address," she

said, tearing him from his thoughts. "There's the Twilight."

"That must be it, over there on the left. That seedy-looking place behind the tavern."

"The sign on the road says Gnash and Gnarly Gym," Annie read, pulling into the parking lot.

"It must have changed hands."

"Which means Randy isn't training at one of Rocko Klugg's training centers."

"That's good, right?"

He laughed. "Hell, I don't know."

The building was a big squat, square conglomeration of light-beige cinder blocks. An orange neon sign glowed *Open* at the double front doors but it appeared the glass inserts had been covered with paper on the inside. A black arrow pointed to the right where a weak yellow bug light illuminated a side entrance. A metal garbage can topped with an ashtray stood sentry at the door and a knot of a dozen or so cars were parked close by.

"I don't see Randy's car," Garrett said as he scanned the vehicles. He gestured for Annie to keep moving, stopping her when they were some distance away, back where they wouldn't be silhouetted against the streetlights.

Annie turned off the headlights as she rolled to a stop but kept the motor running.

"Doesn't look that prosperous, does it?"

"You can't tell with a place like this, especially if it recently changed hands. Maybe Rocko lost the place when he went to prison." He turned in the seat to face her and added, "Will you be okay in the car, Annie? I kind of hate for anyone to associate the two of us."

She said, "I'll be fine."

He pulled the duffel bag out from under his seat, took out her father's loaded gun and handed it to her. "This is the safety," he said. "Leave it on unless you have to shoot it."

"Shoot it! Why would I shoot it?"

"Let's say Curly or Moe tapped on the window—"

"Okay, all right, you made your point. Tell me what to do."

"Flip it like this."

She watched him with enormous eyes. For a second he thought of the way she'd started crying when he gave her the cookie jar. He hadn't known exactly what to do to comfort her. Face it, he hadn't even understood why she was crying. He'd wanted to hug her but after the way they'd touched each other on the sofa, after the difficulty he'd had backing off when he knew he should, he didn't dare. So, he'd stood there like an oaf. And now he sat here looking at her holding the gun she'd carried the first day they met and if anyone had ever looked less comfortable with a firearm, he didn't know who it was.

"Lock the doors, stay in the car."

"Don't worry," Annie said. "Do you want me to drive you closer?"

"No. I want you way back here. I'll walk." He almost added a joke about not accidentally shooting him when he came back but decided against it.

He'd just reached for the door handle when the side gym door opened and two men walked out. The smaller of the men called good night and kept walking to the nearest truck, his breath condensing in the cold air. The second man paused under the light and lit a cigarette, flipping the spent match into the ashtray.

"That's Randy," Garrett said, "all six-foot-four muscle-bound inches of him." He'd dyed his long blond hair a flaming red color, which no doubt explained his wrestling moniker, Red Thunder. He wasn't a bad-looking guy. Expression a little vacant sometimes. He wore a white gym suit the legs of which were licked with yellow and orange "flames."

The other man quickly drove off in his truck but Randy didn't seem to be in any hurry. He took several drags on the cigarette.

"Damn," Garrett said. It wasn't yet seven, so apparently Randy had decided to leave early. Did that mean he'd taken a call from his girlfriend saying someone was asking around about him? Or did it just mean he'd finished training earlier than expected?

"He's huge," Annie said.

"I wonder if he's waiting for a ride." The truth was that Garrett wasn't too excited to approach his old friend in a dark, empty parking lot. If something went wrong he'd have no backup and then Annie would be vulnerable.

As though tired of waiting, Randy smashed his cigarette butt into the sand on top of the garbage can and took off across the parking lot, shifting a gym bag from one big hand to the other. His lumbering gait showed no sign of having sustained a gunshot wound. He'd apparently healed a lot faster than Garrett had.

He held out his hand as though triggering an electronic car opener. The lights came on in a blue sports car that looked like it had just been driven off the showroom floor. Back in August, Randy's ride had been his father's old beater.

"I'll be back in a couple of minutes," Garrett said, pulling on the Stetson.

"Maybe we should just follow him to a place with better lighting and more people," Annie suggested.

He wasn't going to admit he'd entertained the same thought himself. "You don't think I can handle Red Thunder?"

She laughed. "Are you sure you don't want Dad's gun?"

"I already shot him once, I'm not going to do it again."

Garrett walked away from Annie's car as Randy drew even with the sports car. Dressed all in black, Garrett figured he was probably damn near invisible against the dark tarmac. He'd walk slowly, giving Randy time to get half in before he got to him. Hard to run away or throw a punch when trying to fit that much bulk into that small a vehicle.

Randy opened the trunk and threw in the gym bag before moving around the car to the driver's door. At the same moment, the car next to Randy's sprang to life, surprising Garrett, who hadn't realized anyone was inside it. He saw Randy glance over his shoulder at the car, then turn to face it.

A slew of popping noises came next. Randy jerked sideways before disappearing between the two cars. Garrett, who recognized the sound of a silencer when he heard it, ducked down behind the rear bumper of a small truck as the second car squealed rubber and took off. He looked back at Annie's car to make sure she wasn't in any danger, then stood in time to see two taillights flash on as a dark car merged into the traffic and was swallowed by the night. Garrett started running toward Randy, his sore leg all but forgotten in a rush of adrenaline.

Randy lay sprawled on the pavement, his face a pale oval against the sea of shadows on the ground. Garrett knelt beside him. His instinct was to feel Randy's throat for a pulse. He stopped as headlights flooded Randy's upturned face. His brain took an instant photo. Mouth slack, eyes open, blood splatter from the holes in his chest… crimson and flesh…

Garrett choked on a wave of nausea as he lowered his head, his gaze swerving to the car lights, shading his eyes with his hand to cut the glare. He recognized Annie's license plate. She inched forward into the slot vacated by the killer's car. He stood on shaky knees, his gaze back on Randy.

She pushed open the passenger door and leaned across the front seat. "Is he—"

"Yes."

"Get in," she urged.

"I have to call—"

"Garrett, get in the car right this moment. If someone comes out that door, you'll be arrested. Am I getting through to you?"

Knowing she was right and surprised he hadn't realized it sooner, he slipped into the passenger seat, his heart hammering against his ribs, the image of Randy's startled expression burning bright behind his eyes.

She handed him her father's gun and he set it

on the floor. Then she drove more slowly than he could have under the circumstances.

It wasn't until they passed under a street lamp that he saw her hands tremble on the steering wheel.

Chapter Ten

They spent ten frantic minutes trying to think of anything they knew, anything they'd seen that would help the cops find out who murdered Randy. Annie was certain the killer's car was a dark, medium-size sedan and relatively new, but it had been too dark to see any details. Garrett hadn't seen anything except the taillights as they flashed on. Neither of them had seen the gunman or even been able to tell how many were in the car.

As Garrett stepped into the phone booth to report the killing, Annie's cell phone rang. Her caller identified herself as Ellen Boothe. Annie held the phone with an increasingly viselike grip as she listened. On the heels of Randy's violent death, what Ellen Boothe had to say added another layer of surreal shock.

By the time Garrett climbed back in the car, Annie was clicking off her phone. "That was your ex-mother-in-law," she said, meeting his gaze.

The car was dark, his face was illuminated by nothing but the dashboard lights. "Tiffany's been hurt. Someone beat her up. Ellen asked me if I could help with Megan."

"Where are they?"

"At Ellen's house. I promised I'd come right away."

"I'll go with you—"

"Do you think that's smart?"

"I don't care if it's smart."

Annie drove in preoccupied silence until two police cars, sirens blaring, lights flashing, sped past them going the opposite direction, an ambulance on their heels. The official response, for some unexplained reason, caused tears to sting the back of her nose. Maybe she was imagining what the cops were about to find, maybe it was the thought of other innocent people coming out of the gym to find a dead body. She wasn't sure of anything except the fact that for the second time that day, she was in tears.

She pulled over to the curb.

"Let me drive," Garrett said softly. Halfway around the car they met at the trunk and he folded her in a hug. He kissed her forehead before taking her to the passenger door and seeing her inside.

The crying jag was over by the time they turned onto Ellen Boothe's street. As Annie mopped up her face with the tissues she kept in the glove box, she half expected to find more police cars pulled up in front, but the street looked dark and peaceful, the Boothe house closed up, the windows draped. It was the only house on the block without a single Christmas decoration.

"Let me make sure it's okay for you to go in there first," Annie said.

Garrett shook his head. "I've got to see Megan. I'm done hiding. My little girl needs me."

They walked up the path quickly and knocked on the door. It opened right away as though Ellen had been standing on the other side, waiting for them.

"I'm so glad you came. I know it was cheeky of me to ask anything of you but I don't know who else—"

Ellen Boothe's greeting stopped short when she got a good look at Garrett. He closed the door behind them and said, "Hello, Ellen."

Ellen's confused gaze moved from him to Annie. "You know him?"

"Yes."

"You lied to me? You're not from the preschool foundation?"

"No, I'm not. I'm sorry." There was no way to sugarcoat it.

Garrett said, "Where's Megan?"

"She's asleep. Tiffany is in my room. She actually

wanted to see you so I guess it's good you showed up. She's pretty upset, you have to talk to her."

"I have to see Megan first," he insisted. As they all followed Ellen down the hall, Garrett added, "What happened?"

"I'll let Tiffany tell you."

Ellen gestured at a closed door. Garrett opened it. A soft light burned under the room's only window. Megan was tucked into her bed, her curly head all that showed. Garrett quietly stepped over toys and discarded clothes until he got to the bed, stared down at the slumbering child and kissed her head. He came back to the door and said, "Will you stay with her, Annie? I'll go talk to Tiffany and come right back."

"Of course."

Annie tiptoed across the room and gently sat down next to Megan's still form. But Megan wasn't asleep and rolled over as soon as Annie's weight shifted the mattress. She frowned at Annie for a second and then said, "Asia?"

Asia, Anastasia. Annie said, "Yes, honey."

"You come to visit me?"

"Yes, sweetheart. Go back to sleep."

She put her finger against her lips. "Shh, it's a secret."

"What's a secret, Megan?"

"Mommy. She fall down."

"I know." Annie took Megan's hand and squeezed it.

"Asia? I had dream 'bout my daddy."

"Did you really?"

"I want my daddy."

"Guess what, honey? He'll be here in a few minutes, okay?"

The little girl nodded solemnly.

"Maybe if I tell you a story the time will pass faster."

"Okay."

"Maybe a story about cookies. Do you like cookies?"

Megan's smile chased away the tears that had loomed behind her dark eyes. "Tell me story 'bout cookies," she whispered, snuggling close to Annie's leg.

IT HAD BEEN MORE than a year since Garrett had seen Tiffany, but it could have been ten minutes and he still might not have recognized her. Her attacker had gone straight for her face, sparing barely a square inch. Her eyes were swollen and discolored, lip split, cheeks bruised and bloodied. A mass of curls the same color as Megan's tumbled over her shoulders, caked with blood near her forehead.

She opened her eyes when she heard their voices and watched Garrett with drugged acceptance.

"I gave her a little something for the pain," Ellen said.

Turning, he looked down at the older woman. She'd given him his share of grief in the past, but it was obvious seeing Tiffany in this condition had taken the starch out of her sails. Plus, she'd been Megan's main support system for the last several months and for that alone, he was grateful. He said, "Do you mind, Ellen? I need to talk to Tiff."

She left the room as though glad of the reprieve. Garrett sat down on a chair that had obviously been pulled beside the bed for that purpose. The remnants of antiseptics and bandages covered the nightstand.

"Didn't expect to see you," Tiffany said. Her voice was a combination of slurred speech and a lisp caused by the split lip.

Garrett took her limp hand. "What happened, Tiffany? Who did this to you?"

"Two guys," she said.

"Did you recognize them?"

"The one who beat me was bald. The other one stood back and smiled."

He almost said, "Curly and Moe," but of course, those weren't the thugs' real names. One thing was real, though. If Danny hadn't interrupted them the other night, what happened to Tiffany could have happened to Annie. The thought of her suffering these kind of injuries made him queasy.

"Me and Gary rented a little place near the casino," Tiffany said. "Gary is out of town. When I got home, they was waiting for me. One hit me while the other one kept asking questions."

"Did they tell you what they wanted?"

"Papers. Something that belonged to a guy named Rocko Klugg. Something with numbers." She closed her eyes for a second, then added, "Did you give me something to keep without telling me about it?"

"No," he said, his mind racing ahead to the next place they might visit. Why not here? He had to get Ellen, as well as Tiffany and Megan, out of Reno. He added, "I don't know what they want. I'm sorry you got pulled into the middle of it."

She nodded. "Gary will be home tomorrow afternoon and then we're leaving town."

"Maybe you should go now."

"I can't leave without Gary."

"Don't wait too long. Your mother should go, too. Just for a while. Maybe to her cousin's place in California."

"We could give Mom a ride. If Gary says okay."

He swallowed his impatience with her. How could she worry more about some guy than her mother? And what about Megan? He had nothing to offer his child right now. Less than nothing. No home, no permanency. But if he let her leave with

Tiffany he might never see her again. He had to convince Tiffany to leave their daughter with him despite the fact he didn't have a dime with which to sweeten the pot.

He said, "Hear me out, Tiffany. I want Megan."

"Okay," Tiffany said.

"What?" He'd heard her, he just couldn't believe it.

"I can't raise her, Garrett. Mom is sick and Gary doesn't like little kids. He's…well, almost forty-five, he had kids way back when. He doesn't want any more."

"For God's sake, Tiffany—"

"You don't understand," she said, tears rolling from her eyes. "I gotta start over."

A shaft of anger stabbed him in the gut. Now she chose to see the wisdom of allowing Megan to come to him? Now with the world falling apart? Why not months ago before all this happened? "I thought you were under the impression I'm a murderer," he said.

She tried to smile, winced and settled for shaking her head. "I never thought that."

"But you told the police—"

An attempt at a smile made her frown. "I got a diamond earring in the mail and a note that said if I told the cops you would do anything for cash, I would get the matching earring in the mail. You'd already blown Reno so I thought, what the hell. The other earring came a week later. They were the real deal."

Tiffany looking out for Tiffany. She'd been nothing but trouble to him, practically from the beginning, but she was Megan's mother and in an odd way, he knew he owed her more than she owed him. He said, "I'll take good care of her."

"Take her now. Right now. I'll sign whatever papers you want."

"How will I find you?"

"I'll stay in touch with my mother."

"You need to get your mother away before those men decide to check here for some reason."

He didn't think they would, they didn't seem to know he was even in Reno so why bother searching an ex-mother-in-law's home? But why search Tiffany? Why not?

Garrett took one last look at his ex-wife's beaten features. Her injuries would heal, she'd be beautiful again, at least her face would.

"Goodbye, Tiffany," he said, before walking out the door.

She was his past. His present waited down the hall.

"I THINK YOU SHOULD call your brother," Annie said. They'd just resettled Megan in Annie's bedroom. Annie had had to tear herself away from the little girl, but she'd been anxious to hear how it came about that Tiffany allowed her daughter to leave with Garrett.

And then she'd been absolutely horrified by what she heard. Disgusted. She knew some parents were born, some were made, but she'd never run across a woman willing to sacrifice her baby for a man. She would never understand a woman like Tiffany.

Neither of them had eaten dinner and now at midnight, hunger had finally caught up with them both. They shared a can of tomato soup and a sleeve of saltines.

Garrett, swallowing the last of a glass of milk, said, "I won't call Brady." He'd refused wine, said with his family history he had decided when Megan was born to never drink again. She respected that decision.

"Your brother is a cop. He must have experience with things like this," Annie said. "Maybe if you just talked to him—"

"No," he said again, this time with a look that dared her to keep pushing.

She lay her spoon in the bowl, not hungry anymore, and leaned forward. "You need help."

"Not from my brother," he said with another warning glance. He got to his feet and paced the small room, from the television set to the Christmas tree and back again.

"Just explain why," she said calmly.

"I already did."

"Because of your pride," she said. His pacing was getting to her. So was his damn pride.

He stopped for a second and rolled his shoulders, eyes closed, deep in thought. It was one of a hundred of his gestures she was beginning to recognize.

"I don't know how to make you understand this," he said at last, pinning her with his mahogany gaze.

"Just try. Please."

He sat on the edge of a chair. "You have to understand what our house was like. Both parents either fighting or zonked or just plain absent. When I was little, Brady tried to protect me from what was going on. He tried to be my mom and my dad, bailing me out of one mess after the other. He coped by trying to keep everything in control."

"But you didn't."

"No," he said with a deep breath, "I coped by being incorrigible. While he broke his back being the good kid, I went out of my way to be the bad kid. Maybe I was trying to get my folks' attention, I don't know. Anyway, I was in trouble all the time."

"But you're grown-ups now," she said.

"I know. I know." He ran a hand through his hair and added, "I have to handle this myself, Annie. If

I knew how to make sure you wouldn't be hurt, I'd leave with Megan right this minute. But you're in so deep now and the truth is, Megan needs you, too. It's hard enough to admit I need your help to get through this, but I can't turn to Brady until I can face him like a man. Trust me, it has to be this way."

"I know he would help you," she said softly. "He's your brother."

"I know it, too," he said. "But he's a lawman and I'm a wanted man. Think of the position I would be putting him in. I won't, I can't, do it. I'm sorry I allowed you to get so involved—"

"Just stop right there," Annie interrupted. "I'm committed to seeing you cleared of these charges. Don't ask me why, I don't know what to tell you. You and Megan are welcome to stay here as long as you need to. The alternative is you drive off into the night and spend your life looking over your shoulder, and frankly, I care about you both too much to let that happen. I just thought your brother might be able to talk with the police—"

She stopped as he cast her a look that pleaded with her to let it go. She threw up her hands. "Okay. So, why did someone kill Randy? To keep him from talking to you?"

"Nobody knew he was going to talk to me. I mean, I don't think anyone knew. We saw him leaving. He didn't look nervous or anything. I don't know, maybe his death doesn't have anything to do with me."

"Maybe," she said, Randy's bloody face flashing behind her eyes.

"If I hadn't waited around to go talk to him, whoever killed Randy probably would have changed their mind," Garrett said.

"You think so?"

"Most killers don't take chances with eyewitnesses."

She touched his hand in commiseration even though she didn't agree. In her opinion, if he hadn't spent a little time reviewing his options, it was entirely possible he would have been killed, as well. She shuddered deep inside at the thought and what losing Garrett would mean to Megan.

And to her...

Emotionally, she was exhausted. "I can't think anymore," she said around a yawn.

"Why don't you sleep with Megan?" he said, looking at her in that way he had. "I'll take the couch again."

She got up off the chair and moved to stand in front of him. He pulled her down on his lap and she buried her face against his neck as she melted into his arms.

"You should sleep with her," she mumbled against his skin. His beard had passed scratchy and was now soft and so masculine. "She might wake up scared and need you."

"She seemed pretty cozy with you in the backseat tonight," he said.

Annie closed her eyes. She loved the way Garrett smelled. "Do you think when this is over, we can get a horse?" she said.

Holding her around the waist, he settled back in the chair. "You want a horse?"

"Two horses. A brown one like Scio and then another one, any old color will do. We could take Megan riding and have picnics."

"I love to ride," he said.

"You're good with horses," she said. After a moment she added, "What do you want to do when this is over?"

"Do? You mean as in a job?"

"Yeah. Do you want to be a bodyguard again?"

"No," he said.

"What are your dreams?"

"Dreams," he whispered. "Guys like me weren't taught to dream, Annie."

"Everyone has dreams," she said.

He chuckled deep in his chest. "I guess."

"Isn't there something you've always wanted to do?"

"Until tonight, I wouldn't have had an answer

to that question. I've been around violence before, but tonight it was different."

"You mean Randy or Tiffany?"

"Both. Randy shot down in a parking lot right in front of us…" He stopped for a second and Annie knew exactly what he was thinking. The image of Randy's blood-soaked body would be in both their minds for a long time. He finally added, "And Tiffany. What kind of monster does that to a woman? It must have been obvious she didn't know anything. Curly is a sadist, an animal. The thought that it could have been you…"

His voice trailed off, but his grip on her waist tightened.

"So what are you saying?" Annie said at last.

He looked into her eyes. "I'm saying that people like that need to be stopped."

"And you'd like to do it?"

"I think so."

"Like your brother?"

He laughed shortly and then shook his head. "How's that for irony? How do you feel about dating a cop?"

"I've never thought about it before. I would have to give it some serious consideration."

He pulled her closer. "You do that," he whispered, microseconds before his mouth closed on hers. His hands slipped under her shirt and cupped her breasts, his fingers edging under the lace cups of her bra. She dug her fingers into his back and arched toward him about one second away from stripping him naked.

He drew away at the last moment. "You'd better go to bed," he told her, his voice husky and his dark eyes enormous.

Instead she cupped his face in her hands and touched his lips with hers, briefly, playfully, his rough beard a masculine, not unpleasant sensation against her chin.

"Go to bed," he repeated, his fingers stroking her bare midriff before he brought his hands out from under her clothes and straightened her blouse in an oddly endearing way.

"I want you," she said softly.

"Megan is right on the other side of that door," he said.

"I know." She smiled and, licking his earlobe, added, "If she wasn't in the next room and if I got completely undressed and forced myself on you, would you make love to me?"

He laughed into her hair. "I don't know. Let me think about it."

"Answer me now, I want the truth."

"Would you be holding a knife at my throat or anything?"

"Maybe."

"I guess if I had to," he said, his gaze lowering from her eyes to her mouth.

"So, what you're saying," she said, "is that making love to me would be preferable to having your throat cut."

"Yes. That's exactly what I'm saying."

"I just wanted to know," she added. "A girl likes to know where she stands."

He closed the three inches between them and touched his lips to hers again. His hands tightened around her. She returned his kisses with all the longing that swelled in her heart and surged through her blood.

It came to her in a way it had never come before, not ever, not with anyone.

He was it.

Garrett was the man she wanted. She liked him, oh, come on, she suspected she was falling in love with him. She admired him, she desired him, she knew they would be good together, that they would complement one another, that they could build a life. How she knew all these things wasn't as clear as the fact that she did know them.

Which meant unless she got him off the hook with the law, she was indeed going to turn into one of those women who trot back and forth to the prison for stolen moments, stolen kisses, stolen snippets of life.

And that simply was not an option.

Period.

DESPITE THE TERRIBLE happenings of the day before, or perhaps in defiance of the death and destruction, the next day started well. Annie woke up on the sofa to find two brown eyes staring into hers. Megan giggled into her hands.

"Morning, Asia. Daddy says up lazy bum."

"Tell Daddy I need coffee," Annie said.

Megan hurried off to impart the news. After polishing off two fortifying cups, and listening to a half-dozen nonsensical knock-knock jokes, Garrett handed her the newspaper, folded to an inside page. He tapped a short article about the shooting in the Gnash and Gnarly parking lot. There were no witnesses and at the time, police had no leads.

Megan was enchanted by the Christmas tree and insisted on helping Annie rewrap presents, then they spent the afternoon shopping for the must-have replacements for Annie's apartment. Garrett wore a disguise of sorts, his cowboy hat and the leather jacket. But he was out of sorts and grumpy, antsy, only half listening to Annie and Megan's chatter. When they walked past a jewelry store, he said, "Let's stop here for a moment. Let's see if the jeweler can get inside the watch."

Three jewelry stores later they faced the fact that most mall jewelry stores don't have a repairman on the premises. They settled for a boy who claimed his father used to fix old pocket watches and though the boy himself, barely out of his teens, admitted he did little more than sell diamonds to love-struck couples, he offered to take a crack at it.

"Don't say crack," Garrett said, handing the watch over.

The boy grinned. He was six feet of skinny with enough freckles to play connect the dots for eternity. Megan seemed enchanted by him. Annie was beginning to notice that Megan was a people-watcher, a kid after her own heart.

The boy affixed the watch to a suction device and using finesse apparently learned at his father's workbench, twisted off the back of the watch, screwed it back on and took it off and on again just to make sure it worked. He handed it to Garrett with a proud air of accomplishment. After Garrett paid him, they walked out of the store and found an empty bench.

Annie held her breath as Garrett unscrewed the back. She leaned over Megan's head to stare at the spinning gears for a few seconds, finally exhaling.

"Is that how it's supposed to look?" she asked. "All those gears and wheels and little engravings?"

"Yeah, it is," Garrett said.

Megan's tiny finger darted out to touch the fascinating movements that must have seemed like a hidden universe to her.

Garrett caught her hand. "Don't touch it, honey. Sorry." After another few more seconds, he screwed the back on again and met Annie's gaze. "I thought for sure."

"I know. I did, too."

They finished their shopping in preoccupied silence.

On their way home, Annie took a call from Ellen, who wanted to know if Annie had seen Tiffany. Since Annie had never even met Tiffany, Annie assumed the call was for Garrett and passed him the phone.

He listened for a while, his gaze darting between Annie and Megan, his own responses growing increasingly brusque, the tension in his voice building, spreading throughout the interior of the car, resulting in Megan whining and Annie's stomach clenching into a fist. By the time he hung up, it was obvious trouble was brewing. The last thing he'd said into the phone was "Call the local hospitals and the cops."

"You're not going to believe this," Garrett said. With another glance at his daughter, he added, "We need to talk but not in front of the munchkin."

Annie pulled into a fast-food restaurant that advertised an indoor children's playground. They ordered an early dinner and sat near the play equipment as Megan followed a couple of little girls a year or so older than she was on the slides and through the tunnels.

"Okay, shoot," Annie said, popping a hot French fry in her mouth.

Garrett watched Megan for a few moments before starting. "Tiffany decided that since she wasn't getting any money from me, she would try to exhort some out of Klugg. Tell him she would go to the cops if he didn't cough up some dough. So she called the number they'd given her in case she remembered she had something they wanted after all and named her price. Ellen said she tried to stop her."

Annie shook her head. "I thought Tiffany was afraid of these people."

"She was. Last night, anyway. But apparently she got some sleep and greed won out over fear. So, she made the call and an hour later, a woman in her thirties with straight black hair drove up to Ellen's house and picked up Tiffany. Ellen hasn't seen Tiffany since and this was several hours ago."

"Oh, dear."

"I told Ellen to start calling the hospitals."

"Are you thinking the woman who picked up Tiffany at Ellen's house was Jasmine Carrabas?"

Garrett hadn't even unwrapped his hamburger. He picked it up, turned it over and put it down. "The description fits. Ellen is going to go stay with a friend of hers across town. She wanted to make sure Megan was okay."

"I think she wanted to know what to do," Annie said, her gaze drifting to Megan, who stood at the base of a short ladder, still watching the other girls, her face alight with curiosity. "I'm worried about your ex-wife," she added, suddenly chilled through to the bone. She wasn't superstitious, but that chill felt like a premonition.

"I know, I am, too. Damn the woman's greed."

"What about Gary?"

"Apparently she talked to him last night. Ellen said contacting Klugg's goons was Gary's idea. Since Tiffany can't work as a showgirl until her face heals, he told her they owed her."

"Good Lord, they're made for each other."

Megan chose that moment to launch herself into her father's arms. Sitting on his lap, she ate her dinner in fits and starts as Annie watched the two of them, her heart so full of emotion that it seemed heavy in her chest.

The thought that Tiffany hadn't wanted Megan more than she wanted Gary had been so foreign to Annie, so cruel and shortsighted. But the thought that Megan might lose her mother for good, and with it a chance to come to some kind of peace with Tiffany's desertion, was even worse.

Annie took the second call two hours later as Garrett gave Megan a bath. She waited until he'd tucked the child into bed and read her a dozen stories before sitting him down in the living room, making sure with one last peek inside the bedroom that Megan was finally asleep.

"Ellen called," she said, leaning back against the closed bedroom door. "The police called her soon after you and she talked." She paused, trying to think of the right words.

Garrett said, "Just say it, Annie. Whatever it is."

Annie moved across the room to stand near him. "She had just gotten back from the...from the morgue, where she identified Tiffany's body."

He stared at her for a long time, his eyes reflecting shock and grief and anger. He swallowed at last and said, "How did she die?"

"Two bullets. They found her body in a very dark corner of an alley near the casino where she worked. The management there said she'd come in to clean out her locker and get her last paycheck. Speculation is she resisted a robbery as she walked to the front sidewalk to hail a cab."

"Did Ellen tell them about Klugg and Jasmine—"

"No," Annie said. "She's afraid. She's staying

with her friend until she decides what to do. And she told me to tell you she didn't say a word about you to the police."

"I wonder why not," Garrett said. "We've never been what you could call close."

Annie reached for his hand. "I think it's probably because of Megan," she said. "You're all Megan has now and I think Ellen loves her grand-daughter and doesn't want to see her suffer."

He nodded. After a moment or two he added, "Why did Tiffany go into the casino? I mean, think about it. She calls Klugg, Jasmine comes and gets her, then she goes into the casino to clean out her locker? Does that make sense?"

"Let's see. Ellen said Tiffany called there this morning before calling Klugg and told them she was quitting and she wanted her paycheck. She told them she'd been in a minor auto accident and hurt her face. So I guess she then called Klugg, and Jasmine came to fetch her. Let's say Jasmine says sure, we'll give you a little money to keep you quiet. Name your price. Tiffany names a price."

"And insists she be paid in cash," Garrett said. "Jasmine says it'll take her an hour or so to go to the bank. Tiffany figures she'll use the time to take care of business at the casino, and knowing Tiffany, announces this to Jasmine. When Tiffany leaves, Curly and Moe are waiting for her."

"They shoot her."

"In what had to be broad daylight."

Annie shivered again. She remembered the way those two had slinked through the yard at Ben's cabin. The ever-present smile on Moe's face, Curly's solid mass, armed and dangerous, smirking at the thought of death. And poor, misguided Tiffany with dreams of starting over, no match for people intent on shutting her up…for good.

Garrett put his arms around Annie and kissed the top of her head. She held on to him tight. He was so big, so strong, his arms felt safe, his body a bulwark against the evil lurking just around the corner.

He whispered into her hair, his words shattering her moment of peace.

"Randy Larson yesterday, Tiffany today. Who's next, Annie? And what in the hell is Klugg looking for?"

Chapter Eleven

Garrett woke at two in the morning, head pounding. Knowing there would be no more sleep for the night, he got up, dressed in the dark, checked on Megan and came out into the living room, where he settled on a chair next to the sofa on which Annie slept like an angel.

He had to do something. He had to take some kind of action.

He'd woken up with a new thought. What if Greason killed Randy Larson? What if he'd decided Randy, acting for Klugg, had killed Elaine? Would he take matters into his own hands?

Maybe. Garrett didn't know the man that well but he was pretty rich and therefore used to doing things his way and he was mad as a pit bull, so who knew? He thought of calling Greason, but what would that accomplish? What would Greason admit to doing? Nothing. And even if he did admit killing Randy, how would knowing that help?

Always before in his life, Garrett had faced these kinds of problems by packing up his stuff and blowing town. It had been something of a shock when, soon after Megan's first birthday, that's what Tiffany did to him. For the first time he'd been on the receiving end of someone bailing out of a situation they no longer wished or knew how to handle.

He hadn't liked it.

But he hadn't wanted her murdered. She might have been stupid and greedy, but she was Megan's mother. Garrett sincerely hoped Gary spent a long time feeling very bad about his decision to send Tiffany into the lion's den.

Meanwhile, he supposed the next thing to do was go buy a computer cable and charge up the laptop in the miniscule chance Elaine had sent him some kind of information before she died.

Annie made a small sound and his gaze darted to where she slept on the sofa. What he wouldn't give to amble over there and comfort her out of a bad dream. She was getting harder and harder for him to resist, his good intentions all but swallowed up in his increasing need for her.

And that's what it was. Need. Need to touch her, talk to her. She'd become part of almost every thought, her strength something he sensed ran deeper than the sea.

But again, what could he give her besides trouble?

If he could make something of himself. If he could get this all cleared up…

In the end, that sense of responsibility kept him in his chair instead of stretched out on the sofa next to her.

He took out his pocket watch and ran his thumb over the etching on the cover. He'd studied it so often he didn't need a light to "see" the bridge and the water rushing beneath. For a second, he was back twenty-five years, back to a bridge just like that one, Brady always there, too, always protecting him. He folded his fingers over the watch and stared at Annie's shape on the sofa, and in that position, fell asleep again as the sun cast its first rays over the horizon.

He awoke a second time an hour later when the morning newspaper hit the front door. He retrieved it from the top step with a quick look around the frosty, empty yard. No bad guys lurking. So far, so good…and yet there was within him an increasing sense of menace so at odds with the random strings of Christmas lights decorating Annie's neighbors' cottages.

He closed the door and locked it.

By now, Annie was stirring and he moved over to the sofa. Her incredible green eyes glowed as she looked up at him. No woman had ever looked that happy to see him before.

"Move over," he said softly.

She sat up and dragged her pillow and blanket onto her lap as he sat down next to her. As usual, being that close to her made him want her and he grasped her shoulders gently, kissing her before she could turn her face and whisper, "Morning breath."

"You smell like flowers to me," he said against her soft ear.

"Flattery works with me, so keep it up." She glanced at the still closed bedroom door and then at the newspaper. "Any news on Tiffany?"

"I haven't looked yet." They separated the sections. Garrett had just located an article about Randy Larson when Annie read, "Reno showgirl killed during suspected robbery. The body of Tiffany Boothe, 27, who until yesterday worked as a dancer at the Silver Lining Casino, was found in an alley between—"

She stopped reading abruptly as her gaze flashed over his shoulder. Garrett became aware that the bedroom door had opened and turned to see Megan, her new reindeer stuffed under one arm. She ran to the couch and he swooped her up, holding her tightly as her bouncy curls tickled his nose. Annie's lips moved as she continued reading to herself. Truthfully, he didn't have the heart to hear any more about Tiffany's sordid death, especially when the cops were operating without all the facts. He was kind of glad his little girl had provided a distraction.

As Annie and Megan left to get dressed, he read the follow-up article on Randy Larson. When Annie came out of the room, he handed her the newspaper with a meaningful glance at the article, and picked up his baby. "What'll it be, sweetie, cereal or cereal?"

Without glancing up from the newspaper, Annie called, "Just coffee, thanks."

Megan giggled.

WHILE MEGAN WATCHED a Disney video, Annie and Garrett sat close together at the table, their voices lowered. According to the newspaper, police were still investigating Randy Larson's death and thought it might be gang related.

"I wonder if Randy worked for Klugg," Annie said.

"The police won't know to even look his direction," Garrett said.

"Maybe you should go talk to them—"

The muscle in his jaw jumped with tension. "Say I go to them and they discover I've been in town for a few days. Now they find Randy dead and decide I might have wanted to get rid of him. If they ask the right questions, if they haven't already, Randy's girlfriend will tell them a man was calling around asking for Randy the night he was killed. Maybe she'll recognize my voice. I used one of those disposable phones, but still…"

She sat back, hands folded on the table, confused and bewildered.

"Add to that the fact my ex-wife is dead and my little girl, who thanks to Tiffany everyone knows I wanted above anything in the world, is with me. How do I prove I didn't kill Tiffany?"

She shook her head and got to her feet. "I don't know," she said.

"Neither do I. To top it all off, you're in this up to your eyeballs and I am not going to sacrifice you for myself. I need proof, Annie. I need to figure out what Klugg gave Elaine that was so dangerous she used it to blackmail him, what he wants back so badly he's willing to kill for it."

"Tiffany's death might have been just what the police say it was, a robbery gone bad," Annie said. "After all, she'd just collected her paycheck and the newspaper said her purse was missing as well as diamond earrings and a watch."

"The timing is a very handy coincidence. But the police don't know everything we do. If Megan's mother's killer gets away because I didn't come forward, how will I look Megan in the face?"

"You won't."

"Exactly. I have to figure this out and get the information to the cops and make sure Tiff's murderer is caught and prosecuted. For Megan's sake."

"I'm glad to hear you say that. Your brother could help—"

"Don't start that," he said, casting her a fast and furious frown.

She took a deep breath. "Okay, who killed Randy and why?"

He ran a hand through his hair. "I wouldn't be surprised if Greason killed him."

She stopped pacing in front of the kitchen window. "What?"

"If Greason decided Randy killed his wife, I wouldn't put it past the man to take revenge. He drives a black sedan, you know. You saw a black sedan leave the parking lot."

"There are a lot of black sedans…"

He got up from the table. "I'm going to go buy a computer cable and get into the laptop. Maybe there's something there, it's the only stone I can think to turn over."

"And if that doesn't pan out, what next?" she asked.

"Then I'm going to go see Rocko Klugg."

"No!" she said.

He looked at her, eyebrows raised. "No?"

She backed down at once. Who was she to tell

him what he could and couldn't do? Biting her lip, she said nothing.

He kissed her warmly, running a hand down her arm to her hand which he squeezed. "Don't worry about it, okay?"

Her heart beat so fast in her chest it was as though she'd swallowed a hummingbird. That was one promise she couldn't make.

ANNIE STIRRED COLORFUL candy-coated choco-lates into the cookie batter but left out the nuts. She didn't know if Megan liked nuts—many of the children at the preschool didn't.

She hadn't thought about work in days; in fact, it was hard to imagine going back. Who was that Annie who went to work every day and visited with friends and took evening courses at the college? Who was she? And where had she gone?

She knew enough about human psyche to understand she was treading on dangerous ground. She'd let herself get so wrapped up in Garrett's life she'd lost track of her own. Not good. She vowed to call all her girlfriends as soon as this was over and have a big old chick-flick movie night.

There was a knock at the cottage door. Garrett and Megan had been gone for almost an hour and Annie felt her pulse quicken as she went to let them in. Maybe it wasn't good to look forward to seeing them so much, but she did. She'd worry about it later.

Jasmine Carrabas stood on the top step.

Literally speechless with surprise, Annie's gaze flew over Jasmine's shoulder to see if Curly or Moe were lurking behind a bush. Or if Garrett was innocently walking toward the cottage into a trap.

Jasmine said, "I need to talk to you."

"Come in, Ms. Carrabas," Annie managed to say. She had hoped the fake Shelby Parker would flinch at hearing her real name, but the woman was made of sterner stuff.

At least eight inches taller than Annie, Jasmine wore a black leather jacket crowned with a fur-lined hood, black gloves, skintight black pants and boots with three-inch heels. Her black hair was perfectly cut to frame icy blue eyes and very red lips. If Garrett had once reminded Annie of Rambo, Jasmine reminded her of Catwoman.

"What do you want?" Annie said, positioning herself so she could look through the window to keep an eye on the front walk. If Garrett showed up, she'd "accidentally" hit Jasmine with the cookie-dough-covered spoon she still held, and send her to the bathroom to wash up. Her mind raced as she tried to remember just what Jasmine did and didn't know.

"Good, I like people to get to the point. I have a message for you to pass along to Garrett Skye, then I'll be on my way."

Hearing her say Garrett's name startled Annie. "Why do you think I could possibly contact Garrett Skye?"

"A showgirl told me," Jasmine said, eyes glittering beneath black lashes. "She assured me you know how to get in touch with him."

Apparently, Tiffany hadn't told her that Garrett was actually living with Annie. Now it became imperative to get her out of the cottage before Garrett blundered onto the scene as he had the day Vivian came to complain. Annie walked to the door, opened it and said, "I'll give it a try, Ms. Carrabas. Is this message from you or Rocko Klugg?"

Jasmine laughed. "Don't try to dazzle me with what you think you know. Trust me, you know nothing. I'm here simply as a Good Samaritan. Tell Skye to return what he took. Reno can be a dangerous town. No one wants his little girl to suffer the same fate as her mother."

Annie fervently wanted to whack Jasmine with the spoon. The thought of sticky cookie dough plastered in Jasmine's silky hair was delightful. "I'll see what I can do. No promises."

"Try hard," Jasmine said. "For the child's sake.

Give him this number." She handed Annie a business card.

As Jasmine turned to leave, Annie said, "You do realize you're threatening the life of a very small child, plus you've all but admitted Rocko Klugg killed Tiffany Boothe, right?"

Jasmine glanced over her shoulder, one eyebrow arched. "Don't be absurd. What a thing to say." She walked smartly down the front path without looking back, her heels clicking on the cement.

Annie closed the door slowly, looking at the card where she found nothing more than a printed phone number. She walked back to the kitchen where she saw her cell phone sitting on the table.

For several seconds she stood there, motionless, as arguments raged in her head. The pros, the cons, the bigger picture, the fallout. The danger. The life and death danger to herself and to those she loved.

How brave was she?

She put out an unsteady hand.

AFTER GETTING Megan down for a nap, Garrett spent the next several hours picking through his newly revived laptop for some kind of information Elaine might have sent him, something disguised as a file to be downloaded, maybe. He found nothing. He wasn't especially good on a computer anyway and he was having a hard time concentrating.

Klugg was circling in. The only good thing was, it appeared neither Klugg or the rest of his little gang had placed Megan, or him for that matter, at Annie's house. Yet.

Still, Jasmine, acting for Klugg or herself or Santa Claus for all Garrett knew, had made threats against Megan. Tomorrow, one way or another, he was going to get to Klugg and make something happen, no more pussyfooting around, even though every bone in his body ached to grab Megan and make a run for it. But Annie was adamant, she wouldn't run and he wouldn't leave her behind.

There was also a troubling suspicion there was something else Annie wasn't telling him, something that made it almost impossible for her to even meet his gaze and that worried him, too. She'd busied herself in the kitchen for hours, answering questions without elaborating, her usual friendly and outgoing personality closed up like a book.

He was discovering intimacy was an odd thing. Physically, the ways Annie looked and moved were ingrained in his head despite the limited time they had known one another. He bet someone could plunk him blindfolded into a room of a hundred women and he'd know which was one was her just by her delicate scent and the feel of her skin. Her curves, the taste of her lips… They'd yet to have sex but he'd never felt closer to a woman. When this was over, he had high hopes.

But in some ways, she was as foreign to him as the deepest, darkest jungle.

She darted him another look from over her shoulder and this time he decided enough was enough. He got up from the computer and walked to the sink, where she washing up after baking more cookies. The drain boards were piled high with the things.

Putting his arms around her, he leaned over her shoulder and nuzzled her ear. "What's going on?" he asked.

She said, "What do you mean?"

With one hand, he lifted the hair from the back of her neck and kissed her downy nape. "Come on, something is bothering you. Besides Jasmine Carrabas, I mean."

"There's nothing," she said, but she sounded miserable.

He released her, turned himself around and leaned against the counter, arms folded across his chest. "Annie? What's wrong?"

She glanced up at the wall clock.

"Come on, honey, you can tell me. What's going on?"

She rinsed the last bowl and, setting it in the

strainer, turned to him, drying her hands on a dish towel.

"You need your brother," she said softly.

He said, "We've been through this before."

"I know we have. But things are escalating. They know where I live. You and Megan could have walked in on Jasmine today. It's out of control, something has to be done."

"I know," he said. "I know. Tomorrow I'll think of a way—"

She interrupted him by touching his hand. "Let me finish," she said, her gaze sliding to him and away in a manner that left his stomach free-falling. "After Jasmine left here today, I called Brady."

He blinked a couple of times, wishing he'd misunderstood her, knowing he hadn't. He opened his mouth and closed it without speaking.

"I found his phone number on the Internet," she continued. "I called his house. I talked to his wife, Lara. Brady called me back. He seemed very nice. He was relieved to know you're okay."

Garrett pushed himself upright and stalked out of the kitchen. How dare she go over his head and call Brady—

"Hon—Garrett, listen, please. We need help. Two people are dead, three if you count Elaine, murderers are making direct threats against Megan. They all seem to think you have whatever

Elaine took and they are determined to get it back.
I'm scared. You said yourself that the police need
to know what we know if they're going to find
who killed Tiffany. Brady's just coming to back
you up, that's all."

Garrett stopped walking and turned to stare at
her. "He's coming? Here?"

"Of course he's coming."

"When?"

"He'll be here in a few hours."

Garrett ran both hands over his head, linking his
fingers together behind his neck. "Oh, damn it
all, Annie. I asked you not to get involved."

She'd been holding her hand out to him as if in
supplication and now it fell back to her side. She
narrowed her eyes, her expression changed. "Not
involved?" she said. "Excuse me, but exactly how
does a person get more involved than I am right
this moment?"

He shook his head. He'd taken refuge in her
home, he'd put her in danger. But he'd believed
they were on the same page, that she was willing
to give him the opportunity to fix things himself.
A small voice in the back of his head pointed out
he wasn't really doing such a hot job of fixing
anything, but he ignored it. He'd known she didn't
agree with him, but he'd thought in this one area
she'd back off and allow him the decency of

making up his mind when and if to involve Brady. He'd thought she respected him.

The thought of facing Brady with all this garbage hanging over his head just about killed him. He rubbed his eyes and fought the irrational desire to laugh. That desire went away real quick as he imagined the disappointment in Brady's eyes. His brother, Mr. Do-it-by-the-book. Mr. Never-make-a-mistake. Mr. Always-in-control.

Mr. Perfect.

Annie took a few steps toward him. How could anyone who looked so pretty and innocent be so underhanded? So, what was new about that? Tiffany had been a beautiful woman and she'd lied to and manipulated him constantly.

Annie isn't Tiffany…

"I knew if I asked you, you would say no," she said, her chin tilted defiantly.

"You were right."

"I knew your pride would get in the way."

"It must be nice," he said slowly, looking her straight in the eyes, "to know everything."

"That's not fair, Garrett."

"No? Let me tell you what's not fair. What's not fair is you going behind my back." He worked at unclenching his jaw and added, "Call him back. Tell him to stay in Riverport."

There was a very long silence during which

Garrett could hear the drumming of his heart. She finally said, "It's too late for that. He's already on his way."

So that was why she'd kept to herself and then checked the clock before coming clean. She'd been waiting until Brady was on a plane, until there was no way to call him back. For Garrett to avoid his brother now, he'd have to run away like a little kid and he wasn't going to do that.

He swore under his breath and started for the front door. He had to walk off some of this anger before facing Brady.

"Don't get any wild ideas about running," she said and he could hear the false note of bravado in her voice. "If I have to, I'll get a rope and tie you to a chair like you did me."

He paused. Without looking back at her, he said, "Don't you get it, Annie? You don't need a damn rope. You've managed to tie me up without one."

As soon as the door closed behind Garrett, Annie's knees sagged. She gripped the edge of the table for support. The rope thing had been a last-ditch attempt to lighten things up. His return comment had cut her like a knife.

She shouldn't have told him. She should have just kept her mouth shut until Brady knocked on the door. All her confession had accomplished was to give Garrett time to stew and worry.

But she couldn't let him walk into Rocko Klugg's world like he said he was going to. Jasmine gave Annie the creeps and she was just the man's girlfriend. She had to stop him. She'd destroyed the card Jasmine had given her, torn it into tiny pieces and flushed them away. She hadn't told Garrett about a phone number. She hadn't wanted to tempt him.

It hadn't mattered.

"Asia?"

Annie turned quickly to find Megan, clutching her reindeer, standing a foot away.

She kneeled down beside the small girl, smoothing the curls from her forehead, kissing her sleep-warmed cheek. "Did you have a nice nap, sweetheart?"

Megan nodded and leaned into Annie's arms. Annie stood, cradling the child close, gazing down at brown eyes so like Garrett's.

The sad truth was that in her heart of hearts, she'd begun to build a future. Someday she would be Garrett's wife and Megan's mother. Someday. They'd both had some really hard knocks. They needed her. She needed them. Love would grow and blossom and last forever.

The dream was built on quicksand.

"My nose smells cookies," Megan said.

Annie smiled as tears stung her eyes. How could she bear to lose this child? How could she bear to lose Garrett?

HE DROVE IN SILENCE, Annie beside him, Megan in the backseat, singing Christmas carols with mix-and-match lyrics and tunes. He drove down one-way streets and alleys, his gaze darting between the road and the rearview mirror, making a detour into a parking structure and out again just to be sure no one was tailing them.

Since Brady's call from the airport, Garrett and Annie had silently agreed to a truce of sorts, but the tension between them had shifted. It no longer felt as though they were a team. Now they were adversaries, bound together by need. Could it ever go back to the way it was? Did he want it to?

Did she?

"There it is," Annie said, gesturing out her window at a small hotel on the right. Garrett had suggested the place because it had separate entrances to each room from the parking lot, not always an easy feature to find in Reno's big hotel/casino configuration.

It had been Garrett's idea to meet away from Annie's cottage. There was no telling if the place was being watched. They'd left the cottage separately, him through a back window, her carrying Megan out the front door.

Of course, he'd shadowed Annie as she walked along the path, her father's gun loaded and ready in case anyone got tricky. The fear in Annie's eyes as she passed under the overhead lights—fear he was ultimately responsible for—had made him ashamed of himself and that shame further fueled his bad temper.

That and the fact his leg hurt again, reinjured as he ran a half mile to the point where she would pick him up in the car. He'd tripped on an uneven sidewalk, coming down hard on his right leg. The resulting stab of pain had left him breathless.

Brady had called with the number of his room while Garrett raced through the parking garage and now he pulled up in space 113. The door opened before they finished unstrapping Megan from her car seat so they entered the room quickly, Annie carrying Megan first.

The door was quickly shut, the sound of the dead bolt sliding home adding punctuation to the tangible tension in the room.

"It's been a while," Brady said, giving Garrett an assessing once-over. "You grew a beard."

"It comes off the minute I'm not a wanted man," Garrett said. Brady looked the same as he always had.

"Looks good on you," Brady said.

"How's Dad?"

"Believe it or not, in a treatment program. He actually checked himself in," Brady said. He still talked and carried himself as though he knew exactly who he was. He was thinner than Garrett, an inch shorter, his hair a little darker, eye color about the same. He was dressed in jeans and a burgundy flannel shirt, long sleeves rolled up, silver watch, wedding band.

Garrett stuck out his hand. Brady caught it, shook once and then pulled Garrett into a quick embrace that ended with a slap on the shoulder.

"I'm glad you called," Brady said.

Maybe there was something different about him. Maybe it was in his eyes, way back. He seemed a little less formal, a little less guarded than the last time they'd met at their father's house. Garrett said, "You might as well know the truth. I didn't have anything to do with Annie calling. That was her idea."

"You wanted to wait until you fixed everything yourself, right?" Brady said.

"More or less."

"I don't blame you. Still, I'm glad I'm here." He turned then and held out a hand to Annie, adding, "You must be Annie. Thanks for calling me."

Annie nodded miserably and Garrett's heart

went out to her. And then inched away. She'd crossed a line....

Brady patted Megan's curls as he said, "And you have to be Megan. How do you do?"

Megan giggled into her hands. Brady whispered something to her. She nodded, eyes huge, as Brady produced a small wrapped candy which he placed in her hand, closing her fingers around it.

Garrett looked past the knot of people by the door to see a smiling blonde holding a plump baby with the Skye brown eyes.

"Hi, Garrett, remember me?" she said.

He moved past the others to give her a hug. "Of course I do, Lara. Last time I saw you, you were about sixteen. How did my brother talk you into marrying him?"

"I did most of the talking," she said, jostling the baby on her hip. "Meet your nephew, Nathan."

Nathan was a cute little guy, Lara was as stunning as ever. Leave it to Brady to have a healthy, content family. Big brother had done everything right, as usual.

Lara and Megan introduced themselves to each other, then Lara said, "Brady and I took two rooms with adjoining doors. Why don't I take Megan next door with me while you three talk. How about it, Megan, do you want to come with Aunt Lara?

I brought you a coloring book and crayons. What do you think?"

Annie lowered Megan to her feet. The little girl kept hold of Annie's hand. Garrett had never noticed before how alike they looked, both small and delicate with reddish glows to their hair. They weren't related, they'd only known each other for a couple of days, and yet Megan seemed to have accepted Annie as a mother figure. She was too young to understand about Tiffany and he hadn't tried to tell her. He found it astonishing she hadn't even asked yet.

"I'll be right back," Annie said, and then casting him a quick glance, added, "If that's okay with you?"

Now she was asking? He shrugged, unable and still unwilling to mend the rift. He needed time to evaluate what was going on.

Annie and Megan followed Lara through the connecting door. He and Brady stared at each other for a few moments, then Brady said, "Annie is lovely. You're lucky to have her—"

"She's not mine," Garrett said stiffly.

"Oh. I'm sorry. I thought from the way she sounded on the phone that you and she were—"

"Nope. She's a friend. She's been very helpful, but we're not together, not like that."

Brady stared at him a second and then nodded.

"Okay. Come sit down. Tell me what's going on. Tell me what you want."

What? He didn't already have a game plan in motion? That was hard to believe. Garrett remained standing as Brady took a chair. Leaning both hands on the table, Garrett lowered his voice. "I'll tell you what I want. I want to fix myself up with a wire and go talk to the bastard who bombed Elaine Greason and probably killed my ex-wife."

Brady, dark eyes unfathomable, hands folded together, nodded. After a very long pause, he finally said, "Okay with you if I come along?"

Chapter Twelve

"His name is Thorton," Brady said. "He's in charge of the investigation into Elaine Greason's death. I talked to him in August right after you disappeared and I've been talking to him on and off ever since."

Annie saw Garrett's gaze drop from his brother's face to the contents of the paper coffee cup she'd fetched from the urn in the motel office. She wrapped her own hands around a similar cup while Brady ignored his. Not one of them had taken a single sip.

Her heart did a little leap of joy at where she thought Brady might be going with this, but the knot in Garrett's jaw kept her from saying anything. He needed to approach this on his own. She'd done enough for a while. She'd gotten Brady here and he would see to it that Garrett didn't walk into Klugg's house and get himself killed.

As for her future with Garrett? Maybe he would never be able to love her, but at least he'd live.

Megan would have a father. Annie's debt to her own father would be repaid and she would go back to the life she'd led until a week ago.

"What are you saying?" Garrett finally mumbled.

"I'm saying Thorton has had serious doubts about you being the only suspect from day one. Your running away didn't help, and shooting the other bodyguard—"

"He shot me first," Garrett said.

Brady smiled. "Anyway, I think I could arrange a meeting between you, him and the D.A. Annie said you had a tape of Elaine Greason's husband saying this guy threatened him. I think they might be willing to help you with a wire, willing to see if you could get close and—"

Annie jerked so hard the lukewarm coffee splashed onto her hands. "Wait a second. Are you talking about Garrett walking into Rocko Klugg's house?"

Garrett pushed a few napkins her way. "I told you that was my plan."

"But Brady is here now, you don't have to—"

"I have to agree with Garrett on this one," Brady said. "Someone has to get close to Klugg when his defenses are down. Garrett is the one to do it. He can pretend he has what Klugg wants—"

"And what happens to him when Klugg discovers he doesn't have it?" she demanded.

"I'm there," Brady said, "covering his back."

She popped to her feet and stood behind her chair, hands on the back, staring at Garrett. "I thought you were sure the police would blame you for Randy Larson's death or even Tiffany's?"

To her surprise, he laughed. "Listen to yourself, Annie. It's too dangerous for me to talk to Klugg. It's too dangerous for me to talk to the police. What's next? Are you going tell me to take Megan and run? Isn't that where we started? What exactly do you want?"

To Annie's humiliation, the stress of the past several hours culminated in a trickle of very poorly timed tears. She covered her eyes with her hands and struggled to stop them. The next thing she knew, Garrett had folded his arms around her. She attempted to resist, but even though her brain was unwilling, her body wasn't. She needed him. She relaxed against his chest and closed her eyes.

He smoothed her hair, massaged her back, his hands warm and comforting. He didn't kiss her hair like he usually did but his big body was still solid and real. She loved him, she knew that, and she wanted to tell him, she wanted him to know and yet that seemed like just another burden for him to carry when he was almost at a breaking point.

Who was at the breaking point? Who was the one blubbering? She made herself turn away from him. Something told her an undying declaration of love from her was the last thing in the world Garrett would ever want.

"The fact of the matter is this is a dangerous situation with no clear-cut right or wrong," Brady said gently. "But it's Garrett's situation, and the decision has to be his, though someone needs to tell me who Randy Larson is or was."

Garrett said, "What the hell happened to you, Brady? What the hell happened to the man who always knew what to do?"

As the silence continued, Annie turned to look at Brady. She found him staring past Garrett at the doorway of the connecting room. She followed his gaze and found Lara, staring at her husband.

Brady said, "I had a tough year. Thanks to Lara, I lived through it. I guess I learned a little humility along the way."

Lara smiled back at him.

DETECTIVE NED THORTON was a big man in his early fifties with shaggy salt-and-pepper hair and a world-weary air. The D.A. was a woman, younger by two decades, petite and fierce-looking. Her name was Beth Kelly. Garrett had decided against taking a lawyer in with him.

Thorton asked him a thousand questions Garrett

answered truthfully and without holding anything back. He'd committed himself now to this plan.

After a few verbal skirmishes during which everyone made it very clear to Garrett he was not off the hook by a long shot, they listened to what he had to say. Thorton all but admitted he'd had doubts about the validity of the evidence found in Garrett's apartment after he left. The thought of linking Klugg to Tiffany's murder, let alone Randy Larson's, made them both beam.

Garrett didn't mention his suspicion that Robert Greason had been behind Randy's murder. He had no proof and as far as he was concerned, Klugg could hang for everything.

"I did an internship at Elaine's law firm a few years ago," Kelly said after they listened to the tape Garrett had made of his meeting with Greason. She'd dashed off notes during the whole thing. Drumming her pencil against the pad, she added, "I'll tell you right now, I don't believe for a moment Elaine Greason blackmailed anyone. Not a client, not anyone."

Thorton shuffled some papers of his own. "This isn't well-known, but there were a couple of very large deposits made to her account in the weeks before she died."

"Maybe it was her husband's business—"

"No, these were two independently wealthy

people. Her money was hers, his was his. We checked the husband, of course, but his account showed no withdrawals."

"What exactly are you implying?" Kelly demanded.

"Just that it gives credence to a blackmailing theory. We haven't been able to pin down where the money came from."

"She would not do that," Kelly insisted. "It's, it's unethical!"

"You don't know any unethical lawyers?"

"No," she said. "I don't."

He let that pass with a shrug. "Well, Klugg sure seems to think she took something of his," Thorton said.

"True," Kelly said. "But even if Mr. Skye's tape was admissible, which it isn't, it's all hearsay."

Thorton sat back in his chair and leveled a steel-gray stare at Garrett. "So, you want us to wire you and then you want to get in to see Klugg. Is that right?"

"That's the idea," Garrett said. He'd shaved that morning, come out of hiding so to say, and he felt oddly naked. He wore his good quality second-hand jacket and sat there at the conference table a bundle of nerves. If he landed in jail, what would happen to Megan? Brady had assured him that he and Lara would see to it she had a home if it came to that. Garrett did his best not to think of the desolate look in Annie's eyes as she'd heard Brady's assurances. Meanwhile, Brady sat across from him, hands folded. If he was nervous, he knew how to hide it. 'Course, he was a cop, this was common ground for him. And it wasn't his future in jeopardy.

"It might work," the D.A. mused.

"I'll go in with him," Brady said.

Kelly looked at Thorton and said, "Do you think that's wise?"

"The whole thing is a little oddball, but if it works, we might be able to nail Klugg. As it stands now—"

"I know."

Garrett glanced at Brady who shrugged.

Funny thing about this brother of his. He'd always struck Garrett as caring more about how things looked than how things really were, a symptom perhaps of growing up the oldest in an alcoholic family. While Garrett had continued to love and respect his brother, he hadn't much liked him as an adult. Brady had been too rigid. But here they were, actually working together, and Brady was deferring to Garrett every step of the way.

It was little short of a miracle. Of course, once Brady had explained the past year or so of his own life, it was easier to understand this metamorphic change.

Humility. Trust. Learning to depend on someone else. Lara had taught him these things, Brady had told him with a sideways glance at Annie that hadn't escaped Garrett's attention.

"Let's do it," Kelly said, tossing the pad onto the table.

Thorton nodded. "I'll arrange things on this end. We'll have a van out on the street with a receiver and some back-up. Garrett will ask a few leading questions. And Brady, you get him out if things start to go wrong."

Brady grinned at Garrett. "Piece of cake."

THE POLICE PROVIDED a phone number for Rocko Klugg and Garrett made the call on his own cell phone. "He agreed," Garrett said as he clicked off the phone, more anxious than ever to get the whole thing over with. "He remembered me from my visit to prison."

"Rocko Klugg never says anything anyone can use against him," Thorton said. "Don't count on him spilling his guts."

But that's exactly what Garrett was counting on. Resolve coursed through his veins. The police seemed to be trusting him, which in his mind meant they hadn't ruled out the fact he was innocent.

Maybe if he hadn't run that day. Maybe if he'd stuck it out and gotten himself a decent lawyer instead of falling into the old pattern of cutting his losses, maybe this would have all been over by now. The only good thing to come of it was meeting Annie.

The enormity of his rejecting her hit full on in the solar plexus and he took a shuddering breath.

"Let's do it," he said.

DAYLIGHT WAS FADING fast as Brady drove the rental car up to the gate of Rocko Klugg's big white house. The winter landscape and an empty fountain visible from the street gave the place an unlived-in look. Of course, Klugg hadn't been out of prison long; with any luck, he'd be going back soon.

Across the street, a cop in a white jumpsuit worked out of what appeared to be a van, apparently installing a satellite dish to the roof of a neighboring house. Inside the van, officers monitored the wiring apparatus Garrett wore concealed on his person.

Garrett pushed the entry panel button from the passenger side of the car. A voice asked him what he wanted. "Garrett and Brady Skye to see Mr. Klugg."

As the gate slowly swung inward, Garrett glanced at Brady. "Ready?"

"One thing first," Brady said, casting him a level stare. "I don't know what happened between you and Annie Ryder, but take some advice from a man who's been there. Be careful."

"I don't—"

"Don't even try that with me," Brady said. "I saw her looking at you. I know that look. I'm lucky enough to get it every day of my life. Okay, lecture over, let's go."

As Brady pulled up behind a dark sedan, Garrett put troubling thoughts of Annie aside. They would have to wait. His priority now had to be making it through the next few minutes.

He and Brady got out of the car as a man with his hand tucked in his pocket came through the door. Garrett had expected to see Curly or Moe, but this guy was yet another minion, a young man with a know-it-all expression, working hard to make sure Garrett and Brady understood he was armed without actually showing a gun.

Garrett swallowed a boatload of trepidation as he and Brady allowed the man to pat them down. The police had done a good job with the wiring and it remained undetected. Within a few moments, they entered an airy room with huge multipaned windows looking out to the front drive where the last of the fading light cast long shadows.

The room was way too elegant for the man who

sat behind the acre-wide desk. Garrett had seen him once before, of course, in a prison visiting room, behind a thick plate of glass. All and all, preferable to this...

Klugg had been a boxer in his youth and he had the look of one still with a burly build and an oft broken nose. This look was enhanced by a very short prison haircut. He wore heavy framed glasses and over the steeple of his beefy fingers, watched Garrett and Brady walk across the thick carpet. A half-full glass of something amber with a single melting ice cube sat on the blotter in front of him.

He didn't stand as he said, "You got five minutes. Make 'em count."

"I'm here to talk about what you've been trying to get back," Garrett said.

Klugg lowered his hands onto the desktop and zeroed in on Garrett. He wore a very tailored gray suit, a blue tie knotted perfectly around his thick neck. "Go on," he said.

"You threatened Elaine Greason—"

"Old news. She was a lousy lawyer. I said a couple of things when I fired her, I got mad, that's all. Whoever blew her up did the world a favor."

Brady, frowning, said, "Are you saying you haven't been running around trying to get back a document of some kind?"

Klugg's expression remained impassive.

"Something with numbers. A ledger, maybe."

Still no reaction.

Garrett said, "Your girlfriend, Jasmine Carrabas, hired a private eye to find me and then sent two thugs to get back the document Elaine took from you, the one she was blackmailing you with, the one you thought she gave me or that I stole from her before you had her killed. When your thugs couldn't find me or this document, they started a fire to destroy it, just in case I'd left it there. But that wasn't good enough for you. You sent your goons to make sure the private eye's daughter hadn't taken it with her, you searched her house. Then you went after my ex-wife and beat her to a pulp. When she tried to extort money from you, Jasmine lured her out and either killed her herself or set her up for your thugs. One or the other of them probably killed Randy Larson, too. And you threatened Robert Greason. All for this document or this ledger or whatever the hell it is."

Klugg said, "And now you've decided to turn it over to me."

"I never had it," Garrett said. "I want you to call off your goons."

Klugg stood up and looked out the window. Garrett was suddenly aware that another car had pulled up and he caught a glimpse of a woman with shiny black hair pass under the overhead lights.

Klugg turned back to them. His thick lips spread into a nasty-looking smile as he said, "I don't have the slightest idea what you're talking about."

"Are you sure that's the story you want to stick with?" Garrett said. "If that's Jasmine Carrabas I saw through your window, and you let her talk with us, she's going to blow your lies sky-high."

"And how do you know Jasmine?"

"You haven't been listening. On behalf of you and your missing whatever, she's been all over the place."

His small eyes narrowed.

Garrett and Brady exchanged quick looks. They heard a door open and a moment later, a sultry feminine voice called out from the hall. "Rocko?"

"In here," he said.

A moment later, in the process of removing a long, red coat, she walked into the den. "I was in the neighborhood and thought I'd—"

She stopped suddenly, seemingly startled to see Garrett. "What are you doing here?"

"You invited me."

"You were supposed to phone," she said, casting Klugg a quick glance. "I gave that little twit a phone number."

"Don't know anything about that, Jasmine."

"Does this mean you brought—"

She stopped talking abruptly, her gaze shifting from Garrett back to Klugg.

Klugg, taking off his glasses, said, "Go on, Jasmine, continue. It's beginning to get interesting. I'm all ears."

Jasmine pursed her lips and said nothing.

THE PHONE RANG as Annie sat alone at the table, a broken miniature stable scene and a tube of instant glue in front of her. It was one of the keepsakes salvaged from the break-in, given to her years before by her mother. A shepherd's staff had broken in the fracas.

But it was hard to concentrate.

Garrett's drama had gone on without her, that's why she was out of sorts. It couldn't be a broken heart because people don't fall in love in less than a week. The whole thing had been quite an adventure, brought to her courtesy of her long-lost father. But her part in it was over now. Time for real life.

On her way to answer the phone, she ran across Megan's reindeer, left behind when she went with her aunt Lara that morning. Lara had taken Megan and Nathan to an old friend's house, the unspoken message being that it would be better if they were out of Reno for the day. Lara had invited Annie to come along, but

Annie had said no thanks. No point in trying to stay connected. Garrett had made that pretty damn clear.

Anyway, she had to let Megan go.

She had to let Garrett go.

She swooped up the stuffed toy and held it against her chest as she picked up the phone, impatiently flicking away a stray tear or two as she answered.

"Ms. Ryder. Robert Greason here. I'm so glad I caught you. I have a favor to ask."

Annie walked back to the table and slumped once again in her chair, her gaze resettling on the tiny manger. One of the donkey's ears was broken, too, the missing tip no doubt vacuumed up by now. In a dispirited voice, she said, "What can I do for you?"

"I need to get a message to Garrett. I was hoping you could help me."

"I can try. What is it?"

"I believe I found the document Rocko Klugg has been looking for. It's in some kind of code."

"Where was it?"

"In with Elaine's things, at the back of a drawer. I need to talk to Garrett. I think it needs to go to the police."

She was speechless for a second. "I was under the impression you didn't want the police involved—"

"You've talked to Garrett?"

"Well, yes."

"I suspected as much. You're right, I didn't want to damage Elaine's good name, but then I got to thinking about what Elaine stood for. She wouldn't want me bargaining with a man like Klugg. Especially not after he killed Randy."

"You know he killed Randy Larson?"

"I do."

Annie cursed herself under her breath. If she hadn't called Brady, Garrett would have taken this call and not gone to see Klugg and put him or his brother in jeopardy! She'd made things worse by trying to help. Garrett had asked her to stay out of it, but, no, she had to interfere.

"If you get the message to Garrett to meet me at the house—"

"Oh, but he can't, at least not right away. He's talking to the police about Rocko Klugg."

"He went to the police?"

"Quite a while ago now."

After a long pause, he said, "What a shame I couldn't get this to him earlier. I'm coming into town for a meeting tonight so I'll drop it by the station myself. I just thought it might be better for Garrett if he was involved."

Maybe it would be. Maybe this was a way to make up for calling Brady. "I could come get it," she said.

"No, I'm on my way out of the house. But you'll be seeing Garrett?"

Why deny it now? She said, "Yes."

He paused for a second, perhaps readjusting what he thought he knew with the current information. He finally said, "If you want to get it to Garrett, then we'd better meet somewhere. How about the casino where I work? The Glistening Sands? I'll leave an envelope with my secretary, twelfth floor."

"Okay."

Annie immediately called Garrett's cell. Maybe she could get to him before he went to see Klugg. Maybe there was time to abort the visit until the police had had a chance to review this new information.

The cell rang twice before clicking over to voice mail. Swallowing her disappointment, she left a message then grabbed her purse and coat and flew out the door.

As usual, the Christmas traffic made it a slow trip. An hour later Annie took the elevator up to the twelfth floor of the Glistening Sands. It emptied directly into a wide reception area with a desk set at an angle. The colors of the walls and carpeting were all muted grays and blues, a peaceful, almost oceanic atmosphere at odds with the glitzy, noisy casino over which it hovered.

The place was abandoned. The lighting was subdued as though everyone had gone home for the day. She walked around the desk and looked for a note or a package, but could see nothing. It hadn't occurred to her to ask Greason what form the "document" was in so she didn't have the faintest idea what she was looking for.

As she was about to start searching for somebody to help her, a door at the far end of the corridor opened and a man appeared. He looked to be about fifty with silver hair and brilliant-blue eyes. He smiled at Annie and said, "Are you Ms. Ryder?"

"Yes. And you're—"

"Robert Greason."

Annie said, "I thought you had a meeting."

"I do, I do," he said. "But Caroline, my secretary, had an emergency so I decided to wait for you myself. Some things are more important than meetings, right?"

"Of course," Annie said.

"Come on back and I'll get the book." He disappeared through the door.

So, the mysterious document was in book form. She entered a spacious office geared as much for entertaining as working, the city visible through the huge windows a mass of twinkling lights far below. Greason stood behind a narrow desk, opening a drawer.

"Come in," he said. "Ah, here we are."

He held out a notebook for Annie who moved closer to take it, suddenly aware of footsteps coming down the hall.

Greason glanced over her shoulder. "Ah, there you are Wilkins. You're right on time."

Annie turned to face the newcomer.

Chapter Thirteen

Jasmine Carrabas stood silently while Klugg had Garrett repeat everything he'd said before, using almost the same words.

When he was finished, she casually draped her coat over the back of a leather wingback chair and sauntered to Klugg's desk, where she perched on the edge, picked up his watery drink and tossed it down.

But Garrett saw her hand shake. And now he noticed the skin around her mouth looked pale and taut, her eyes shifting, assessing.

"Tell me about the private dick," Klugg said.

She flipped her free hand as though it was all of no consequence. Putting the glass back on the blotter, she slid off the desk, leaned down and kissed Klugg, then started back toward the door.

"Jasmine?" At the sound of her name, she stopped and turned back to face Klugg. "Tell me about Mr. Skye's ex-wife."

Garrett narrowed his eyes. Crazy as it seemed, Klugg sounded genuinely confused.

"Tell me about this thing they say you keep telling them I want back. What exactly is it, Jasmine? 'Cause, you see, the funny thing is, I never gave Elaine Greason anything but a fat paycheck she didn't deserve. And I never threatened her besides that once when I fired her. So, what's going on?"

Garrett's gaze swerved from Jasmine to Klugg. "You never threatened Elaine?"

"Like I keep saying, when I fired her, sure, the damn broad took my money and delivered zippola. But afterwards, what am I, stupid?"

"But the phone calls—"

"Don't look at me," Klugg said.

"And following her at night, sending dead roses—"

"Please. Children's games."

"When I came to the prison to see you, you didn't deny any of it," Garrett persisted.

"Why should I bother? Who are you or the Greasons, for that matter? Nobodies. If someone was threatening Elaine, good for them, let everyone think it was me. Good for my image. 'Course, now I got a new lawyer and a new trial coming and I'm supposed to clear all this up." He looked back at Jasmine and said, "Tell me what you know. Now."

Jasmine raised one perfect eyebrow. "I'm not going to answer questions like this, Rocko." She glanced at her watch and turned to walk out.

In that instant, Klugg rose from his desk clutching a .357 Magnum revolver he'd apparently pulled from a desk drawer. Jasmine seemed to feel it aimed at her back, for she turned at once, her eyes growing very wide at the sight of it.

Brady said, "Put the gun away, Mr. Klugg. There's no need for violence."

"Talk," Klugg said to Jasmine, ignoring Brady.

Garrett heard a few words of double-talk before he tuned her out.

Why would Klugg disavow making threats? He wouldn't. He'd be proud of them unless he was acting, but Garrett didn't think he was.

So who made the threats using Klugg's name?

And why? To scare Elaine and Robert Greason, why else? To get them to hire a bodyguard and take precautions. And the bigger question, the jackpot question. Who put the bomb in Elaine's car, who pushed the button, who killed her and framed him?

Was it really Randy? Is that why he had to die? But if that was true and he was working for a killer, why not get rid of him months ago, why wait until Garrett got back to town?

Garrett searched his mind. Who, of the people

involved in this mess, knew he was in Reno besides Annie? Tiffany's mother, but she was lying low. Tiffany herself, the last day of her life, anyway, but by then this current drama was well underway. Who else?

One person. Only one. One person who also knew Randy, who had access to Garrett's apartment. One person who knew Garrett's background, his familiarity with munitions, for instance, because he'd had access to Garrett's employment file.

One person.

What if Garrett's stomachache the day Elaine had been blown sky-high wasn't the result of the flu, but something more sinister? What if Greason had doctored Garrett's food or the lemonade only he had imbibed the night before at the party? Elaine had said she was celebrating that last night. Was she celebrating blackmailing her own husband? If so, why?

He said, "How well do you know Robert Greason, Ms. Carrabas?"

She instantly fell silent as the blood seemed to drain from her face.

Garrett looked at Klugg and said, "I think you're being used, Klugg. I think your girlfriend is in cahoots with Elaine's husband to kill Elaine and blame the whole thing on you. And me." He shook his head at his own foolishness. How had he been so blind?

How had Elaine? But why?

"Why?" he asked Jasmine.

Klugg said, "Is this true?"

"Of course not," Jasmine said. She managed a laugh, but even Garrett could tell she was faking it.

"My boys told me you were running around," Klugg said, glowering. "They just didn't know with who."

With a toss of her head, Jasmine said, "You're going to believe this guy?"

Klugg all but growled. In a derisive voice, he snarled, "Can Robert Greason afford you, Jasmine? You don't come cheap."

She looked down her nose at Klugg and said, "You needn't worry about that. He's got millions."

Millions? Since when? Garrett thought. Had Greason stolen Jasmine away with a false fortune? The man was wealthy, but millions?

Klugg swore. Brady took a step toward him. "Why don't you put that gun back in the drawer, Mr. Klugg? There are cops—" That's as far as he got.

A shot thundered through the room. Jasmine flew off her feet and landed on the carpet with a sickening thud. Brady immediately lunged for Klugg, who dropped the revolver as though it burned his hand.

Garrett pulled out his cell phone. He could hear the sound of running footsteps and shouts coming from outside.

Annie didn't answer her phone. She always answered her phone. He checked for a message. There were two. One from her. And one from Robert Greason with a simple request....

ANNIE'S HEART shriveled at the sight of the man Greason called Wilkins. *Curly*.

Greason, moving to stand between Annie and the doorway, addressed Wilkins, "Where's Spencer?"

"He left a while ago," Curly said.

Irritation flashed across Greason's face as he barked, "Go back downstairs. As soon as you see Skye, bring him up here. Make sure you check him for a weapon."

Wilkins left.

Why was Greason giving Curly/Wilkins orders? And why was Garrett coming here? As her mind raced, Annie thumbed quickly though the notebook. The pages were blank. She slapped it on the desk and said, "What's going on?" with the sickening feeling she already knew the answer.

"Let's just say it's the end of the line, at least for you and Garrett Skye," Greason told her.

He withdrew his hand from his pocket. The gun he pointed at her wasn't huge, but it had an ugly matte-black finish. Annie flinched. "That man works for you," she whispered as though a loud noise might make the gun explode. How she hated the things. "And Jasmine Carrabas? Does she work for you, too?"

He carefully walked behind her to his desk where without taking his eyes off her, he picked up the desk phone and pushed a button. It didn't take long for him to say, "Jasmine, it's me. Call." After he hung up, he added, "Actually, Jasmine and I enjoy a more intimate relationship."

"Klugg didn't hurt anyone," Annie said, struggling to readjust her thinking. "Klugg is innocent—"

"Innocent? Rocko Klugg? Hardly. There's little doubt he had his business associates eliminated and probably the hit man he hired to do the job, as well—"

"But not Elaine."

"No."

"Or Tiffany."

"A singularly stupid and greedy young woman."

"Or Randy."

"Technically, the only one I killed myself," he said.

Despite the alarm that raced through her veins like Paul Revere's call for action, there also existed a morbid curiosity. So many people had died. For what? "You were afraid Randy would tell Garrett what he knew," she said slowly. "He planted the car bomb at your instruction."

"And was paid well for doing it. The only other thing he had to do was shoot Garrett the next day. If he'd been a better shot, the cops would have arrived to find their prime suspect dead, case closed and wrapped up with a bow."

"You hired Garrett just to frame him for killing Elaine," Annie said. "You sent him to Nevada Prison to talk to Klugg to establish an opportunity for Klugg to hire him. You must have convinced your wife Klugg was after her."

He smiled as he said, "You should have seen her face when she opened the dead flowers."

His chuckling glee repelled her, but it also made him seem infinitely human and flawed and actually steeled her nerve a little. She said, "Garrett was out of the way. No one knew where he was, you were safe. Everyone thought he did it, you'd paid off Randy. Why hire my father, why not just leave things be?"

"I didn't know about the damn safety deposit box," Greason said. "When I searched Elaine's things and found nothing, I assumed she'd already destroyed the evidence."

"What evidence?"

Ignoring her question, he picked up the receiver

once again and impatiently placed another call to Jasmine Carrabas, leaving the same message as before. Annie could tell from the way he fidgeted he was getting nervous. But the gun remained aimed at her heart, and if there was a more gripping way to feel naked when you were clothed, she didn't want to know about it. Her mind shifted to Garrett and what awaited him when Curly got his big hands on him, but she pushed it away. If she allowed her thoughts to touch on him or Megan, she knew her bones would dissolve and she'd puddle on the floor.

Greason took a deep breath, his gaze darting between Annie and the office door. He said, "My wife was a selfish bitch."

Annie didn't respond. She could think of nothing to say that wouldn't antagonize him.

"She thought she could bleed me dry while all the time presenting the loving wife crap to the world. But I showed her."

Annie couldn't help herself. "Then the black-mail part is true, only it wasn't Klugg, it was you she was blackmailing. Was it really a document of some kind?"

"Yes."

He'd mentioned a safety deposit box he didn't know about. Little question about which box he meant. Shelby had said she cleaned one out months after her mother's death, which must have meant her name was on the box, not Greason's. She said, "That's when this started, isn't it? When Shelby cleaned out her mother's box at the bank."

He shrugged as though her knowing anything made little difference to him. "She called me when she got back to Tempe. She'd seen the contents before, she thought there might be things missing. She checked with the bank and found out Elaine had visited the box the day before her death. She wanted to know if I knew anything about it."

"So you went down to Arizona for a visit but what you really wanted was to see if whatever Elaine took from you was in with the other things."

He appeared startled Annie knew about that trip. He said, "The contents were just Elaine's brother's junk."

"And you got worried Elaine might have given something to Garrett, so you hired my dad to find him. And now two more people are dead and you still don't know if what you're so desperate to get back is out there somewhere or destroyed in a fire."

His smile this time was as cold as his eyes. He said, "You'll appreciate the irony. Just this morning, out of the blue, I received a bill from Elaine's favorite jewelry store. They'd done some work for her but had delayed billing in deference to her shocking murder."

"So?"

"So now I know what I'm looking for. I called Garrett and asked him to deliver it to me, told him it was sentimental. You better hope he still has it or you'll end up like your father."

She grew very still. "What do you mean?"

He looked as though he was about to deliver the punch line to a joke as he said, "Your father got nosey and investigated Jasmine." His lips twitched as he added, "So, he had to go."

"What do you mean he had to go?"

"I mean, he insisted on the truth. The truth has no place in business."

"You killed him?"

"Jasmine did. She called him and arranged a meeting. There are drugs that mimic heart attacks—"

One minute Annie was standing there, mouth open, listening to this fiend rattle off a list of the people he and his little gang had knocked off and the next, she'd launched herself across his desk, hands out, aiming for his throat, heedless of the gun. And she reached him, too, probably because he was too startled to react as quickly as he should have. The gun flew out of his hands as she gouged at his throat and eyes and anything else she could reach…

Until he managed to swing an arm and slap her back against the desk, onto the floor where she landed on her rear end. She screamed something at him as she popped to her feet, ready for a new attack, but he'd recovered the gun and held it pointed at her, his expression grim.

"You little tramp!" he spat, wiping blood from his face with the back of his hand. She'd scratched his left cheek so hard she'd broken a fingernail and left fiery tracks through his skin. "The minute Skye gets here, you're dead."

He'd as good as killed her father. He was planning to kill Garrett. Swallowing tears for them both, she looked Greason in the eye and spoke from the heart. "I hope you rot in hell."

LUCKILY, BRADY had left the keys in the ignition of the rental. Garrett drove in a frenzy to the Glistening Sands. He parked in a quasi-legal spot and all but ran into the casino, slowing down only when he noticed his actions were causing people to turn and watch.

He made his way to the elevator at the back, the one designated for casino business. He was unarmed and, of course, he should have waited for police backup or taken Brady or even told someone where he was going, but he'd reacted out of pure gut instinct. His woman was in danger and, worse, it was his fault for involving her. For loving her.

For pushing her away.

I'm coming Annie, he thought for the hundredth time in the past twenty minutes. He'd once told her he knew that love was thinking of another person's happiness before your own, about whether you made life better for them or only made things worse. But it was more than that, he knew now, it was also being willing to work out differences, to give the one you love a chance, to forgive and glory be, to be forgiven.

He was hopelessly in love with Annie Ryder. He'd been a jackass. He'd hurt her because of his insufferable, selfish pride. And if she suffered because of his shortsightedness, he would never forgive himself.

He had to make sure she knew he loved her and that none of this was her fault.

The elevator opened and he entered it half lost in thought, his brain spinning with plans. He knew what Greason wanted, he just didn't know what would happen when he found out he'd made a mistake.

As the door closed, a huge, pale hand grabbed the edge and tried to force it open.

Garrett's response was immediate, made on a level of consciousness he wasn't even aware of. He slammed down with both hands, knocking the man's grip loose, but recovery was swift, and this time the intruder used both his hands, spilling a glass of something clear and cold in the process. Garrett caught one quick glance at the man's face—Curly—before he kicked up with his right knee in the jerk's groin. The man fell forward onto his knees and Garrett knotted his hands together. He brought them down on the back of the guy's head like a hammer hitting a nail dead-on.

Miracle of miracles, Curly fell flat on his face.

Garrett gave him an additional punch just to be sure, then quickly dragged him into the elevator, where he frisked him. He recovered a Beretta and a spare ammunition clip. As the elevator doors closed, he yanked off Curly's necktie and used it to bind his hands behind his back. Having worked in the building, he knew of an employee restroom on the eighth floor and detoured there.

The floor was deserted, office workers long since gone home for the night. Garrett hadn't noticed he'd reinjured his right leg until the adrenaline wore off. Dragging a big man like Curly was hard work. Once through the restroom door, he dropped Curly's thick shoulders onto the tile floor. He made sure Curly didn't carry a cell phone, then stripped him of his belt and used it to tie his ankles. He stuffed Curly's socks into his mouth to keep him quiet.

Outside the bathroom, he jammed a chair under

the door handle. Curly wasn't going anywhere for a while.

The elevator smelled like gin, explaining what had been in the spilled glass. As he rose the remaining distance, he checked out the Beretta, his throbbing leg keeping time with his heartbeat.

He stuck the gun in his waistband on the off chance Greason hadn't alerted Annie to any danger. No reason to up the stakes if he didn't have to. Maybe she could walk out of here. He'd like to walk with her; man, he had a million things he wanted to tell her, a million apologies. She'd asked him once about his dreams. He should have told her the truth, only at that time he hadn't known it.

I've been dreaming my whole life of finding you, he should have said.

The blasted elevator dinged when it reached the twelfth floor. So much for stealth. He rethought his decision to go in without the gun in his hand. Pulling the Beretta, he exited the elevator, but the game was up before it started.

Greason stood in front of his secretary's desk, an easy target except for the fact he held Annie in front of him, a gun against her throat.

Garrett tensed at the sight of her, at the hopelessness stealing into her eyes. Her right index finger was bloodied at the nail, her jacket was torn, her hair fell around her face.

"Drop the gun," Greason said.

He'd acted like a man too in love to use his head and the result was a standoff with Annie in the middle.

Greason looked behind Garrett, probably for Curly. Greason's urbane polish was gone, ruined by the four red scratches running down his left cheek and the disarray of his silver hair. "I said drop the gun. Where's Wilkins?"

"All tied up," Garrett said, assuming Curly's real name was Wilkins.

"For the last time, take the clip out of the gun, put the gun on the floor and kick it over here. You know what's at stake."

Annie. Annie was at stake. Garrett met her gaze briefly before following orders.

Greason made Annie pick up the useless gun and drop it into his pocket. That chore taken care of, he looked at Garrett again and said, "Did you bring it?"

"Yes."

"Put it on the desk."

"Don't do it," Annie said with the defiant tilt to her chin. "He killed Elaine. Damn, he killed everyone—"

Greason twisted her arm up behind her back. Annie screamed out in pain. Garrett took a step forward, stopping when Greason jabbed the gun against Annie's throat hard enough to create a dimple in her skin. "Now!" he shouted.

Garrett pulled out the pocket watch.

"The watch?" Annie said, her voice reflecting the same doubt Garrett felt upon hearing Greason's phone message, requesting its return.

Greason said, "Unscrew the back."

Garrett said, "I've already looked inside. It's just an old fashioned windup watch."

"It's been modified by a jeweler to look and weigh the same as the original but with a hidden electronic movement," Greason said anxiously. "Even though the winding stem seems connected, it's just a ruse. Look beneath the old movement. There should be a digital camera memory card tucked in there, a tiny little thing."

Garrett recalled Elaine snapping pictures of the letter opener in Lake Tahoe and then putting the small camera in her purse. Later she'd taken the purse into the bank and then emerged with the books, cuff links and watch taken from the box she'd shared with her brother. She'd given the items to him, and that night she'd celebrated. If she'd lived long enough, she probably would have asked for the watch back, but she thought it was Rocko Klugg threatening her; she didn't know it was her own husband and that her time was limited.

Not a marriage made in heaven.

"What did Elaine take pictures of?" Garrett asked.

Greason said, "Shelby found out Elaine used the bank's paper shredder that day. Obviously after she'd photographed my ledgers, she wanted to get rid of the copies she'd made of the originals." He watched hungrily as Garrett unearthed the tiny blue metallic chip.

"You're an embezzler," Garrett said. How else to explain Jasmine's claim of millions, especially when it included "documents" over which he'd killed three people.

"An embezzler?" This from Annie.

"He has to be." Garrett studied Greason and added, "I didn't think you were stupid enough to steal money from a casino."

"Put the card on the desk." When Garrett paused, Greason twisted Annie's arm tighter again, jabbed the muzzle of the gun even deeper. Annie gasped as tears sprang to her eyes. Garrett quickly put the chip on the desk.

"Pick it up, put it with the gun," Greason said. Annie did as told, pain etched on her face as Greason kept a tight grip on her contorted arm.

"They'll kill you if they find out," Garrett said.

"You should probably be more concerned with your own fate," Greason said. Motioning with the Beretta, he added, "The door to the stairs is on your right. You go first. Keep in mind what happens to the girl if you try anything."

Garrett searched for options. Rush Greason, Annie gets shot. Refuse to move. Ditto. There was still hope. As long as he kept his eyes open…

As he started to turn, he gaze collided with Annie's. "I love you," he whispered, or maybe he didn't, maybe he just thought it.

The stairs led to the roof. "Over there," Greason said with a nod, gesturing toward the edge. There wasn't a place to hide even if that opportunity presented itself, there wasn't anything to pick up and with which to mount an attack. Nothing.

"I assume you want us to jump," Garrett said when they'd reached the railing. It was a windy, cold night, the moon hidden behind thick clouds. Despite still being wrapped in her purple jacket, Annie shivered, probably from fear as much as from the cold. Light from the overhead fixture streaked her auburn hair as it blew across her face.

"I'd rather be found with a bullet hole in my head than let him get away with this," Annie said, facing him.

There was that defiant chin again. You had to admire a woman who could act ballsy three feet from a thirteen-story drop with a gun pressed against her throat.

Garrett, smiling to himself, said, "I agree."

"But that's not the way it will happen," Greason said. "You can either jump together, a tragic but fitting end for a desperado like you and the woman he seduced into helping him, or Annie can take a bullet in her leg, in her hand, in her foot, in her belly until you, Garrett, put an end to it by jumping. It's up to you."

"It's going to be kind of hard to convince anyone I killed myself with Annie full of holes. Oh, by the way, did I mention Rocko Klugg shot and killed Jasmine an hour or so ago?"

Greason's initial bark of disbelief petered out when Garrett returned his stare without flinching. He said, "That's not true."

"Yeah, well, Rocko felt jilted when he learned about her two-timing him with you. You better watch your back."

As he talked, Garrett moved a step closer. He could sense Greason's distraction as the man attempted to discern the truth of Garrett's claim. And then Garrett saw something shift in Greason.

"Get my cell phone out of my left pocket," he told Annie. "Slowly." She reached into his pocket with her left hand and awkwardly retrieved the phone.

"Flip it open, punch speed and one."

She did these things as well.

They all heard a man's voice ask who was calling. It sounded a lot like Detective Thorton to

Garrett, but the noise of the wind made it hard to tell. It sure as hell wasn't Jasmine.

"Turn it off," Greason demanded, "and drop it." She did those things, too. Greason kicked the phone out of the way.

All the implications of the situation seemed to hit him at the same time. Jasmine dead or captured. The futility of murdering Garrett and Annie, the fact the police would easily trace the call just made to Jasmine back to Greason.

Garrett said, "It's over. Let Annie go."

Greason actually released Annie who, gulping, cradled her arm and took a few halting steps toward Garrett as he reached out for her. But then Greason seemed to change his mind. The gun rose from his side, pointed at Annie's back. The light of madness glazed his eyes.

"Down!" Garrett yelled, his last image of Annie her frightened face as she twisted away.

Garrett dove for Greason's legs as the gun fired. He sensed Annie collapse as he wrested the gun from Greason's fingers and sent it flying. He hit Greason in the face a couple of times, then stopped, catching his breath, catching his wits. Before he could roll off the other man, shadows fell atop him and he looked up to find two large men, heavily armed, standing over them.

One lifted Garrett to his feet as though he was

a child. He held Garrett's arms behind his back and Garrett got his first good look at the other man.

Moe. Curly's accomplice.

Oh, no…

Garrett 's heart plunged even further as he caught sight of Annie's still form a few feet way, almost lost in the shadow cast by Moe's stocky torso. Was she alive or dead? Garrett struggled to get loose, not because he thought he had a chance of overpowering the brute who clutched him but because he couldn't bear to be restrained when Annie's life might be ebbing away.

Moe said, "Let go of him, Tony."

Garrett's captor released his grip. For a second, Garrett was too stunned to move.

"Take care of the girl," Moe said. "We'll take care of Mr. Greason."

With the none too gentle help of the man called Tony, Greason got to his feet. He shrugged his arm free and straightened his jacket. "What the hell is going on?" he shouted, rubbing his cheekbone. "Shoot the bastard," he added, pointing at Garrett.

Instead, Tony whacked Greason on the head with the butt of the gun.

Dumbfounded, Garrett limped to Annie and knelt by her side. She lay on her back, staring up at him, clutching her arm.

"Oh, God, Annie—" he said as he ripped off his jacket.

"I don't think it's too bad," she said, glancing down at her arm. Moe had moved and now she now lay in a pool of light. She blanched as she saw her own blood seeping between her fingers. He immediately covered her with his jacket.

He took out his phone to call an ambulance as the two men, Greason between them, disappeared through a different stair door.

What had happened? Moe worked for Greason, so why was he giving orders instead of taking them? Garrett fought the urge to pick up Annie and make an escape before Moe and Tony changed their minds and came back. But he didn't know how badly Annie was hurt and he didn't want to take a chance. He settled for recovering Greason's gun.

Annie smiled up at him, her eyes a little unfocused.

He kneeled again. "Hang in there, honey. I'm calling…"

"Wait." Lips trembling, tears rolling off her face into her hair, she said, "Before you summon the troops…I…I want to say I'm sorry…"

"No, honey, it's me…"

"No, listen. I love you. I understand how you might not want me. It's okay." Her lips trembled as she mumbled, "I just want you and Megan to be happy."

Garrett heard footsteps thundering on the stairs. He looked up in time to witness the door thrown open and Brady appear. His brother looked around, zeroed in on Garrett and Annie. He started running toward them.

Garrett had two seconds before chaos descended.

Two seconds.

He smoothed the tears from Annie's face as he leaned over her, touching his lips to hers.

"Marry me," he said. "Be my love forever."

Epilogue

Megan called it the "I do," ceremony, and Annie supposed it was as good a name as any.

Theirs took place the following autumn, after Annie's arm healed, after Garrett's leg was cared for properly and he'd graduated from the Oregon Police Academy, after she'd moved to Riverport to join him and Megan and make a home.

As the orchestra began playing, Annie looked around the beautiful parklike setting. This property had once held the house Lara Kirk grew up in. Now it was the new site of a teen center under construction, the land donated by Lara's mother to the city after her house was destroyed in a fire. The grounds had been painstakingly reseeded and were now lush, the towering maple trees that had survived the fire turning gold with the coming of cooler weather.

But this day was perfect. Temperate, almost balmy, a salute back to summer, and Annie took a deep breath of river-tinged air, filling her lungs with promise.

Sometimes she had nightmares, but not the ones she'd expected. Not of being shot, not of being hit on the head or scared out of her mind. Not of losing Garrett. Oddly enough, her nightmares revolved around Robert Greason being led away by two men, one of whom she would forever more think of as Moe, off to who knows where, never to be heard from again until his body washed up in the Truckee River a month later.

Police investigation pointed to a mob connection working for the casino. Garrett had been right. The casino found out about Greason's embezzling and took action of their own, planting Moe there as an informant, their main objective getting their money back. Needless to say, Moe seemed to have disappeared off the face of the earth. Curly had been as clueless as he appeared to be.

But that was the past and the future was so close.…

Annie's mother, dressed in lemon yellow, came around the corner of the partition erected to give Annie privacy before the ceremony. "It's time, honey," she said, smiling broadly.

Time.

Annie took a deep breath and followed her mother. They were greeted by Garrett's father who held Megan's hand. Annie had met the elder Skye a dozen times on her visits to Riverport. He kissed her cheek before placing Megan's hand in hers and proceeding to escort Annie's mother to their seats.

Annie had heard the horror stories about Charles Skye, of course. But the man she'd gotten to know was gentle and best of all, a nondrinker, charming with his grandson and doting on Megan.

"This time for real, Asia?" Megan asked. She was dressed in soft yellow, the same color as the highlights in her ringlets. She held a white basket full of gold and orange rose petals. For days the little girl had been rehearsing tossing petals whenever Annie moved. There wasn't one intact flower at their new house.

Annie said, "This is the real deal."

The orchestra began playing the wedding march, and Annie, dressed in white but without a veil covering her eyes, leaned down and kissed Megan's cheek. "Are you ready to become my little girl as well as Daddy's little girl?" she whispered.

Megan, nodding, giggled into her hand, then turning, began the walk. Annie followed in a blizzard of petals.

The first person she saw was Vivian Beaumont Ryder Perkins, sitting with her new husband, the wealthy octogenarian she'd stolen from her aging mother and who had ridden to the rescue, checkbook in hand, and paid off Mox before disaster struck.

And then there was Lara, standing on the left side of the altar, facing her, a woman Annie had come to love as a sister and with whom she would soon work at the teen center. Teens loved cookies, right? She would be a big hit, Brady teased her, if she kept baking.

Across from her, on the right, Brady smiled at her and her heart seemed about to burst. *A sister and a brother.*

At that moment, Garrett stepped in front of Brady and turned to face her. The tears started as his dark eyes scanned her face and gown, registering approval and desire. Why did she always have to cry at the worst possible times?

As though he knew exactly what she was thinking, Garrett politely covered a laugh with a little cough. But that ended as she got closer and he reached out his hand. Their fingers touching ignited an invisible shower of sparks. Megan stood between them.

As the preacher started speaking, Megan tossed the rest of the petals into the air, where they floated down on Annie's and Garrett's upturned faces.

The little girl cried, "I do," as loud as she could. And they did.

* * * * *

The Colton family is back!
Enjoy a sneak preview of
COLTON'S SECRET SERVICE
by Marie Ferrarella,
part of
THE COLTONS: FAMILY FIRST *miniseries.*

Available from Silhouette Romantic Suspense
in September 2008.

He cautioned himself to be leery. He was human and he'd been conned before. But never by anyone nearly so attractive. Never by anyone he'd felt so attracted to.

In her defense, Nick supposed that Georgie could actually be telling him the truth. That she was a victim in all this. He had his people back in California checking her out, to make sure she was who she said she was and had, as she claimed, not even been near a computer but on the road these last few months that the threats had been made.

In the meantime, he was doing his own checking out. Up close and exceedingly personal. So personal he could feel his blood stirring.

It had been a long time since he'd thought of himself as anything other than a law enforcement agent of one type or other. But Georgeann Grady made him remember that beneath the oaths he had taken and his devotion to duty, there beat the heart of a man.

A man who'd been far too long without the touch of a woman.

He watched as the light from the fireplace caressed the outline of Georgie's small, trim, jean-clad body as she moved about the rustic living room that could have easily come off the set of a Hollywood Western. Except that it was genuine.

As genuine as she claimed to be?

Something inside of him hoped so.

He wasn't supposed to be taking sides. His only interest in being here was to guarantee Senator Joe Colton's safety as the latter continued to make his bid for the presidency. Everything else was supposed to be secondary, but, Nick had to silently admit, that was just a wee bit hard to remember right now.

Earlier, before she'd put her precocious handful of a daughter to bed, Georgie had fed his appetite by whipping up some kind of a delicious concoction out of the vegetables she'd pulled from her garden. Vegetables that, by all rights, should have been withered and dried. She'd mentioned that a friend came by on occasion to weed and tend it. Still, it surprised him that somehow she'd managed to make something mouthwatering out of it.

Almost as mouthwatering as she looked to him right at this moment.

Again, he was reminded of the appetite that hadn't been fed, hadn't been satisfied.

And wasn't going to be, Nick sternly told himself. At least not now. Maybe later, when things took on a more definite shape and all the questions in his head were answered to his satisfaction, there would be time to explore this feeling. This woman. But not now.

Damn it.

"Sorry about the lack of light," Georgie said, breaking into his train of thought as she turned around to face him. If she noticed the way he was looking at her, she gave no indication. "But I don't see a point in paying for electricity if I'm not going to be here. Besides, Emmie really enjoys camping out. She likes roughing it."

"And you?" Nick asked, moving closer to her, so close that a whisper would have trouble fitting in. "What do you like?"

The very breath stopped in Georgie's throat as she looked up at him.

"I think you've got a fair shot of guessing that one," she told him softly.

* * * * *

Be sure to look for
COLTON'S SECRET SERVICE
and the other following titles from
THE COLTONS: FAMILY FIRST *miniseries:*
RANCHER'S REDEMPTION
by Beth Cornelison
THE SHERIFF'S AMNESIAC BRIDE
by Linda Conrad
SOLDIER'S SECRET CHILD
by Caridad Piñeiro
BABY'S WATCH *by Justine Davis*
A HERO OF HER OWN *by Carla Cassidy*

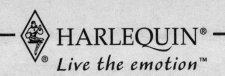

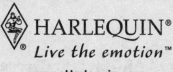

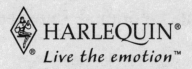

HARLEQUIN®

Super Romance®

...there's more to the story!

Superromance.
A *big* satisfying read about unforgettable
characters. Each month we offer *six* very different
stories that range from family drama to adventure
and mystery, from highly emotional stories to
romantic comedies—and much more! Stories
about people you'll believe in and care about.
Stories too compelling to put down....

Our authors are among today's *best* romance
writers. You'll find familiar names and talented
newcomers. Many of them are award winners—
and you'll see why!

If you want the biggest and best
in romance fiction, you'll get it
from Superromance!

Exciting, Emotional, Unexpected...

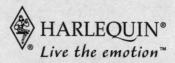

HARLEQUIN®
Live the emotion™

HARLEQUIN®
Presents®

**The world's bestselling romance series...
The series that brings you your favorite authors,
month after month:**

Helen Bianchin...Emma Darcy
Lynne Graham...Penny Jordan
Miranda Lee...Sandra Marton
Anne Mather...Carole Mortimer
Melanie Milburne...Michelle Reid

and many more talented authors!

Wealthy, powerful, gorgeous men...
Women who have feelings just like your own...
The stories you love, set in exotic, glamorous locations...

HARLEQUIN®
Presents®

Seduction and Passion Guaranteed!

Harlequin® Historical
Historical Romantic Adventure!

*Imagine a time of chivalrous
knights and unconventional ladies,
roguish rakes and impetuous
heiresses, rugged cowboys
and spirited frontierswomen—
these rich and vivid tales will
capture your imagination!*

*Harlequin Historical . . .
they're too good to miss!*

Silhouette

SPECIAL EDITION™

Emotional, compelling stories that capture the intensity of living, loving and creating a family in today's world.

Special Edition features bestselling authors such as Susan Mallery, Sherryl Woods, Christine Rimmer, Joan Elliott Pickart— and many more!

For a romantic, complex and emotional read, choose Silhouette Special Edition.

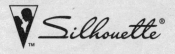

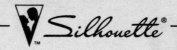

SPECIAL EDITION™

Emotional, compelling stories that capture the intensity of living, loving and creating a family in today's world.

Modern, passionate reads that are powerful and provocative.

nocturne

Dramatic and sensual tales of paranormal romance.

Romances that are sparked by danger and fueled by passion.